THE GRAYSTAR THEORY

THE GRAYSTAR THEORY

VIRGIL BALLARD

READERSMAGNET, LLC

The Gray Star Theory
Copyright © 2018 by Virgil Ballard.

Published in the United States of America
ISBN Paperback: 978-1-947765-53-5
ISBN Hardback: 978-1-947765-76-4
ISBN eBook: 978-1-947765-54-2

All rights reserved. No part of this publication may be reproduced, stored in a retrieval system or transmitted in any way by any means, electronic, mechanical, photocopy, recording or otherwise without the prior permission of the author except as provided by USA copyright law.

No lines, parts and quotations was taken from other books or any previous publications.

The opinions expressed by the author are not necessarily those of ReadersMagnet, LLC.

ReadersMagnet, LLC
10620 Treena Street, Suite 230 | San Diego, California, 92131 USA
1.619. 354. 2576 | www.readersmagnet.com

Book design copyright © 2018 by ReadersMagnet, LLC. All rights reserved.
Cover design by Ericka Walker
Interior design by Shieldon Watson

CHAPTER 1

He desperately wanted to make a good impression but the conversation had lagged and he was at a loss as to how to keep her interest and attention. Jason was a somewhat timid 28-year-old with a tall, lanky physique, curly blonde hair, and thick, black-rimmed glasses. He worked as a bookkeeper for Allen Enterprises, a large corporate office that developed and managed technological ingenuities. It wasn't his dream job, but it paid enough to live a semi-comfortable life and allowed him to keep to himself despite his curious, playful nature. On this particular day, as mid-morning drifted anxiously into late afternoon, Jason had summoned all of his courage to ask his co-worker, Sarah, to lunch.

Planet earth had always held its boring days, and Sarah yearned for something more. Allen Enterprises, although a very successful business model, was like any ordinary corporate job. It employed thousands of people in a large, eight-story building, and the level Sarah and Jason both worked was on the third floor. The area was a tortuously long and broad maze of cubicles, offices, and gray painted walls. It was much like any significant company floor with a hierarchy of its populace. The grunt workers were jam-packed in the labyrinth of cubicles while the higher up personnel procured large, glass-windowed offices around the floor's perimeter. Sarah and Jason both worked in cubicles, but were fortunate enough to have adjoining partitions that lay in close proximity to the employee break room.

Having always had a difficult time in social situations, Jason hid inside his comfort zone, not wanting to stand out in any way. Being average to him was satisfying enough even if it made him almost invisible. Jason had been pleased with his efforts in managing to come out of his shell a bit over the past eight years while working in the large office, quelling his paralyzing shyness upon discovering he had a unique ability, a talent you might say, that others did not possess. At this point, Jason had guarded the knowledge of his talent zealously, not wanting to draw attention. Besides, he could not explain it.

Jason, like many of his peers working the robotic repetition of a mediocre job, wanted a more fulfilling life. His cubicle neighbor, Sarah, had been hired just a month prior, and every day since first catching a glimpse of the beauty, he felt compelled to learn more about her. He felt a magnetic pull toward her that he had never experienced before, as if the universe wanted him to meet her, know her. It was the first time in Jason's life he felt this way, and he witnessed a tinge of anxiety pulse inside him, being very apprehensive at the unfamiliarity of new territories. He knew that Sarah probably had no idea who he was and perhaps she felt awkward about being the new employee. Jason knew despite his fear that it was up to him to make the initial contact. So far, the only connection the two had ever made was when Jason calmly waved to Sarah while they had walked past each other in the hallway. Luckily, she had acknowledged Jason with a half-hearted but welcoming smile. However, if he ever expected to get more than just a friendly "hello," Jason knew he had to make the effort. His heart raced as he did everything within him to muster the confidence to approach Sarah.

On this particular day, a sun shining, clear blue summer, Jason rehearsed his lines, dressed his best, and made all efforts to act natural in his environment. Sarah was getting a cup of coffee in the employee break room, her second in the first hour, when Jason made his approach.

"Do you take cream with that?" he asked, standing next to her while beginning to prepare his own coffee cup.

Returning a brief smile, Sarah replied, "No, but thank you." Jason felt a lightning bolt of nervousness surge from head to toe. He knew this was not the time to walk away or appear uneasy in Sarah's presence. He gulped a breath, exhaling self-assurance.

"My name is Jason. I'm a bookkeeper here and a really nice guy. Would you like to go to lunch with me today?" The quick delivery and hastened breath made his tension much too obvious.

It may have been an abrupt method, but Jason waited, smiling, for an answer.

"I know who you are, Jason. My name is Sarah and I would love to have lunch with you. How does noon sound on the fifth floor?" Jason grinned eagerly. She was not only beautiful but had a great sense of humor. She was also very accepting of his apprehension despite being completely confident and poised herself. It was obvious that Sarah was referring to having lunch in the Allen Enterprises cafeteria located on the building's fifth level. Noon was the time all Allen employees were able to take a half hour lunch break. Jason nodded his head with visible joy, excited that Sarah had accepted his lunch date proposal.

Jason felt it was still a legitimate date despite the time and location, but now, sitting across the table in a small corner booth, Jason's timidity overwhelmed him and he became withdrawn. Perhaps it was the face-to-face contact. He couldn't tell for sure. Sarah talked briefly, allowing Jason to get to know her better, but she noticed Jason wasn't saying anything at all. It was almost as if he was not even acknowledging her. The two sat in silence a moment while Jason pushed rice and kung pao chicken back and forth across his plate. With Sarah expecting him to contribute to the conversation, he was now beginning to appear less than timid, but downright rude. Perhaps out of desperation, he, knowing she was watching, acted without thinking. He angled his fork upright with the tines pressed into the plate and the handle facing the ceiling. He let go of the fork, and it slowly began to rise, stopping at about four inches above his plate. It remained motionless, suspended in time. Sarah looked at the fork with a stunned gaze. She was now the one who was speechless. Jason did not notice. He leisurely dropped his hands below the table and onto the napkin in his lap. He then raised the paper napkin in both hands, slowly dabbed his mouth, and placed the napkin back upon his knees. He then reached out in front of him and retrieved the fork, taking a bite of his food as if nothing happened. Only then did he look up to catch Sarah's eye. He had her attention alright. Sarah sat mesmerized with her mouth agape, not able to believe what she had just witnessed.

"How did you do that?" she asked emphatically. Jason smiled, hesitated, and then took on a very serious look. He peered around him repetitiously, examining the ceiling as if searching for hidden cameras, then leaned close to Sarah, looking directly into her eyes.

He gave his first reply of the lunch date in a very serious, low voice, "I'm sorry, I can't talk about it." Jason had no idea where this would lead, and not being one to fabricate a story, he was certainly swimming in uncharted waters. Sarah, being a new employee with the company and having known Jason for only a short while, was not alarmed but intrigued. Was Jason some sort of magician? She took the action and answer to be a challenge to a duel of wits and began to identify that this behavior was the type of expressionism Jason was most comfortable with. She accepted the match. Luckily for Jason, Sarah was a very open-minded and spry character and was not in any way afraid of what Jason had just demonstrated. In fact, she was almost honored that Jason would share such an amazing feat with her. After all, she was merely someone he had just officially met. Sarah was also desperate for adventure and excitement, something to separate the ongoing monotony of day to day life, and this seemed to be a perfect introduction to such a longing.

Sarah was a perky 25-year-old with long, red hair, green eyes, and a fair complexion. She had graduated from a prominent university with a degree in journalism just two years prior. Her passion was reporting, researching, and writing, but she had been unable to find employment in her field. She had accepted her present position at Allen Enterprises as a receptionist/secretary while vowing to find a way to live out her dream. Allen was just a temporary position. Sarah, not knowing if her acceptance of Jason's remarkable act would discomfort him, responded quickly, "I'm sorry, Jason. Sometimes I think I see things that aren't really there. I guess it could be because of who I am. But anyway, if what you just did with the fork is real, it is an amazing feat. I am hoping we can get together again but…if you are spoofing me somehow…I wouldn't like that…" She paused momentarily then continued, "Could you do it again just so I know it's real." Jason just shrugged and ignored her request. Sarah had hoped her response would ease his evident anxiety, but she didn't know quite how to achieve this, and it was clear that Jason was becoming more and more embarrassed. A few minutes passed in silence as the pair ate the remainder of their lunch.

As Jason stood up to leave, Sarah offered her hand saying, "thank you for the lunch." Jason smiled broadly and gripped her hand firmly. He wanted to like her, and also for her to like him, but he wasn't sure if he was doing things right or at least not completely obliterating them. His fear told him to walk away, but the kindness in him emerged the victor and he turned toward the table as he rose from his seat, palm faced out as a gentlemanly gesture. Sarah slowly rose to his outstretched hand. She warmly put her arm in his as they walked to the elevator, and without saying a word, Sarah signaled to Jason with her body language that she wanted him to know that she accepted him. What may have seemed initially an inept first date had ended up fostering an inexplicable chemistry neither Jason nor Sarah had ever known.

For the rest of the afternoon, Sarah could think of nothing else than the unassuming, book-geek that had some sort of mysterious, out-of-this-world ability. She sensed that Jason liked her and admitted to herself that he wasn't too bad of a guy. She was also captivated by the challenge of his demonstration that was something he obviously kept secret. She had accepted the challenge, and after a couple of days of mulling over various plans, decided to create her own mystery for him, but she knew she had to think fast. Sarah caught herself daydreaming over the next few days, biting her lip and sweeping the smooth hair from her face. The plan had to be good. She had to make Jason believe she was ready to take on any type of challenge, no matter how indescribable or bewildering.

CHAPTER 2

Sarah's college roommate, with whom she had remained close friends, had an older brother, Bob, who was known to be quite a jokester. He had assisted Sarah before on a couple of occasions arranging extravagant practical jokes. She was sure she could count on him if she needed his help and felt satisfied with her quickly laid out plans to challenge Jason. It only took a couple of smiles before Jason asked her out again the following week. This time, it was a request for a dinner date.

Jason began feeling as though Sarah understood him and he was appreciative of the fact that the power he had shown her had not scared her away, but rather attracted her to him. Stepping up his novice dating skills, Jason planned a more romantic and glamorous date. He dressed in a button-up shirt with a tie, the only one he owned. He put a dollop of hair gel through his pale tresses, slicking it back rather than letting it fall over his eyes like usual. Sarah, with giddy excitement, chose a bright red dress to accent the hair suspended neatly on the top of her head. She tried on several pairs of shoes, fruitlessly determining which worked the best, and settled on a pair of classic, black high heels. Jason picked her up at her place, just three blocks south of Allen Enterprises in the heart of the city.

Like a perfect gentleman, he bowed and kissed Sarah's hand upon opening the front door to him. She blushed with a blissful grin and the two exchanged greetings. She was all ready to go and locked the door to her house as she exited. She stuck the key in her small, black purse, and then they walked hand-in-hand to Jason's car. He opened the door for her, made sure she was comfortable, and then started the engine. So far, Jason was feeling much more self-assured than usual.

Jason had given himself a serious pep talk before picking up Sarah, not wanting the petrifying silence of timidity to take over him once again. He pledged assertion and confidence within him, at least to the best of his ability. He found his attraction to Sarah growing immensely with every day they saw each other, each word they spoke, and savored the time they were spending together.

Jason drove to a popular steakhouse, *The Brand House*, where they started with a more fluid conversation and a bottle of red wine. The night began with the typical small talk, both Jason and Sarah learning more about each other while feasting on juicy steaks and seasoned vegetables. They sipped wine and found compatibility in each of their personalities. About an hour into the evening, Sarah waiting for the opportune moment where Jason appeared to feel more relaxed, leaned forward and confided a secret.

"Jason, there is something you should know about me…" She looked down almost as if embarrassed. It rolled off her tongue hastily, "I'm a hybrid." She pointed to a black dot on the fleshy part of her left hand between the thumb and forefinger. It looked very much like a tattoo, but was small enough to be mistaken for a dark freckle. Jason scrunched his face in wonderment, pulling in closer to investigate her hand.

"What do you mean by hybrid?" he asked uneasily. She placed the dotted hand in his to give him a better look.

"Well," she answered, beginning a pragmatic approach to her story. "Believe it or not, my mother was an alien abductee and impregnated while aboard a flying saucer." She then looked Jason directly in the eye, smiled sweetly, and waited. His first thought was that she was kidding him, creating some farfetched story, but he really had begun developing feelings for this girl and decided to play along. Sarah withdrew her hand.

"How are you different?" As he waited for her response, he began to cut into a piece of medium-rare steak.

"It's hard to say," Sarah replied, "But I do know the MIB are watching me."

Surprised, Jason swallowed hard, "MIB?" he questioned. Sarah acted casual, natural, and continued to speak between sips of wine.

"Yes. You've heard of the men in black, haven't you?" Well, yes, he had heard of the men in black, but he gave them no credence at all.

Jason took a moment to chew before playfully and sarcastically responding, "Yeah." Surely she was having some fun inventing this crackpot story. Perhaps she was doing it to make Jason more comfortable with having revealed his power, but he did not need it now. He understood Sarah's acceptance and almost felt that his power was solely responsible for Sarah's developing fascination with him. He decided to drop the subject and continue dinner discussing other topics.

After dinner, dessert, and few more drinks, Jason paid the bill. Sarah sat with her chin cupped in between her hands, not taking her eyes away from Jason's except to blink. She appeared smitten and wasn't afraid to show it. She gawked as he paid the bill, smiling back at her every so often, and finished his glass of wine. Like a perfect gentleman, Jason then escorted Sarah back to the car, walking unhurriedly with hands clasped softly.

"I really like you, Jason." Sarah admitted calmly. "I've had a great time tonight."

Jason agreed with Sarah's sentiment, but his attention abruptly changed course from his beautiful date to a suspicious-looking man loitering in the steakhouse parking lot. The man was perceptibly watching them, smoking a cigarette next to the main entrance of the restaurant. Incidentally, the man was dressed in all black, including dark sunglasses and a thick black hat. Odd. Why would a man be wearing sunglasses at nighttime? Jason decided not to think too much of him and shrugged off the coincidence of the man in black that had been in his line of sight just moments after Sarah had revealed to him that she was being watched by them. Jason giggled internally, for the man was very young and portly, features Jason found inane for the fictionally fearsome men in black organization. Jason opened the car door for his date and began to drive. The couple continued to talk, still feeling like they were beginning to open up further to each other as Jason drove back to Sarah's house. When Jason led Sarah to the threshold of the front door, the two shared a long, wonderful embrace.

CHAPTER 3

"Thanks, Bob!" Sarah exclaimed as she hung up the phone. It was Monday and Sarah was running late for work. Luckily, the young woman thrived on chaos and knew how to make the best of bad situations. She enjoyed simplicity, but she also reveled in the moments when she could experience any form of excitement in her life. She treated every day like a new opportunity, even though she had recently been feeling depressed over the lack of her passion for investigative journalism. Sarah, however, was resilient to her negativity and was able to focus and create fulfilling opportunities for herself. Her newfound companionship with Jason was leading to feelings Sarah had never experienced, and she felt delight each time she would go to work and pass by his cubicle.

As Monday morning passed, then noon, both Jason and Sarah were waiting for each other to make a move. Neither had spoken to each other that day, but there had been complex dialogue in their passing facial expressions. By three o'clock, Sarah was standing at the counter in the break room, fixing another addicting cup of coffee when she felt her skirt rise, exposing a shapely thigh and panty line. Quickly pulling it down, she looked around behind her and spotted Jason smiling. His gaze was stably placed upon her, and she was the one to finally break the verbal silence.

"Aren't you a sneaky one?" she quipped.

Jason chuckled lightly and confessed, "Well, I just couldn't resist."

Once mere co-workers, Jason and Sarah had both distinguished that together they had begun to advance a romantic relationship. It was growing with each glance, each day, each laugh shared, and inexplicably, each time a prank was pulled on the other. The relationship thrived on jokes, pranks, and convivial hoaxes.

More and more time passed as the pair continued to spend time with each other. Within a couple of months, Jason officially began calling Sarah his girlfriend. Likewise, Sarah began addressing him as her boyfriend. The relationship had begun to take full bloom, but Jason's powers were not a part of it. Sarah felt as though Jason should embrace his power and learn to vocalize and emote using his gift. Similarly, her journalistic instincts constantly shaping, Sarah began to press Jason to allow her to write a story about his power to share it with the world. She imagined it to be a half investigative journalistic story and half an interview with the sensation himself. But Jason steadfastly maintained his desire to keep his unique power low-key and within reach. He didn't necessarily believe it needed to be kept a secret, but Jason did not enjoy flaunting his abilities for all of mankind to judge. He liked sharing it with people who appreciated his power like Sarah did and also with the people he felt most connected to. Jason did, however, agree with Sarah to experiment with his talent. Jason had no idea what his limitations were and had only recently began discovering the truth of his power. The capabilities of the power were mostly unknown to him, and Jason had not continued to demonstrate or talk about them since the couple's first date in the cafeteria. However, Jason had to admit, levitating a fork sure was a good icebreaker.

Jason knew from the time he was a little boy, first learning to understand his identity and significance in the world that something about him was different than others. He didn't know exactly why and had not a notion as to how different he was until he was twenty years old.

Jason had had a wretched childhood. He lost both his parents at a very young age, was an only child, and grew up with an older cousin who scorned the child relentlessly. Jason was also extremely shy, tentative, and quiet. He had difficulties making friends or expressing himself despite being remarkably smart. He succeeded in all subjects at school, but fell behind while in high school due to bullying, poor home life, and ostensible cowardliness. Puberty had been an exceptionally difficult time for Jason. His face had been riddled with acne, he was scrawny and disproportionately tall, and he was utterly self-conscious. He never had a girlfriend or best friend to confide in throughout his teenage years. In fact, he really had no friends at all. Even if some of his peers attempted to befriend him, Jason felt compelled to push them away. It also didn't help that his cousin was unaccepting and callous toward him. By eighteen years old, Jason dropped out of high school and moved into his own place. For two years he attended school online, receiving his high school degree and getting certification in accounting while working as a night janitor to support himself. He spent many days in solitude, but was content in his self-made reclusive confines.

Just two days after his twentieth birthday, Jason was at work one day, mopping a large tiled floor, when he felt extremely fatigued. Thinking he would be unable to finish his work, he stood up wearily with mop in hand, leaning against the wall. The water bucket was placed about twenty feet away and required several steps and physical strength to move it over to his location. So exhausted, Jason could only stare at the bucket. But as he stared, concentrating and wishing it would just magically come to him, something amazing happened. Jason's determined attentiveness made the bucket begin to wiggle until seconds later it slowly and gradually slid roughly across the floor. Interestingly, Jason was not alarmed or amused by the occurrence. Instead, he was thankful, and didn't think much about his achievement. He continued to use his newfound ability a little bit at a time, beginning to believe that the power was a unique skill that possibly no one else possessed. He had never heard of anyone else being able to accomplish the menial tasks he had been able to control so easily, at least not in real life. However, Jason was never directly interested in what this gift meant or entailed. He mostly used it for fun when he was bored or when he wanted to get something done. It had never been used for good or evil and exhibited no tangible significance.

It wasn't until Sarah persevered that Jason began to experiment with his power more and more, concentrating deeply and learning that his skill was based on manipulating energy. It seemed his effective levitation range was about 15 to 20 feet, but it depended greatly on weight. The heavier the object, the slower and less distance he could move it. Jason tried lifting himself with some rather interesting results. He could just clear the ground, but couldn't seem to levitate more than an inch or two. Jason was able to discern that his weight, approximately 165 pounds, was directly correlated to the distance he could levitate. Jason also discerned he could stand on a chair, step off, and slowly sink to the floor at a rate of one inch per second. He hypothesized that with just the weight, the heavier the object falling, the faster it would descend. Jason began journaling his progress and discoveries, wondering if the unique idiosyncrasy of his power was merely influencing gravity. Sarah encouraged him to continue to work on his understanding of the talent, and that with practice, the powers would likely strengthen and adapt. It wasn't long before he was able to do other things with his power, and that this otherwise meaningless talent was blossoming into a full-fledged gift. The reward, however, was not developing his powers into usable skills, but sharing his growth with Sarah.

It was evident to Sarah that Jason was becoming very comfortable and trusting with her, something that at first did not seem like an undertaking he would be able to accomplish so easily. However, Sarah did not confess to Jason that the story about the MIB was a hoax, and that the dot on her hand was nothing more than an extremely dark birthmark. The only thing she even knew about the MIB was the famous movie "Trifecta" and the "Conspiracy Theory" that a faction of men who were possibly aliens in disguise would kill you if you attempted to unlock the mysteries of space. Sarah did, however, tell Bob to stop appearing as a MIB. She had recruited Bob to entertain the joke that Sarah was a hybrid human-extraterrestrial and that the men in black were stalking her. Bob insisted he had only posed as an MIB once, when Sarah had first asked him, which was at the steakhouse entrance where the couple had enjoyed their first dinner date. It was also the time Sarah had shared her mysterious hybrid tattoo and exposed that men in black were watching her. When Sarah found out that Bob had stopped posing as a MIB, she couldn't help but notice how often she and Jason were encountering them. She had assumed Bob was dressing in disguise or employing his own friends to pose as MIB to continue the rouse, but Bob was adamant that he had acted alone and only one time. Sarah wasn't much of a worrier and figured there was a good explanation for the black-frocked men that kept catching her eye around town or just considered it to be a wonderfully weird coincidence.

Sarah and Jason continued experimenting with his energy, manipulating abilities for weeks and beginning to realize how much fun they could have by surprising unsuspecting people with friendly pranks and gleeful gags.

The couple were sitting on a park bench one warm, sunny afternoon when a man came walking by. He was dressed in all black, another serendipitous encounter, and looked quite out of place as his high-glossed shoes clicked on the paved walkway. As he approached, his black hat suddenly lifted straight up, exposing his balding head. The hat stopped at about two feet in the air and began to slowly rotate. The expressionless man stopped mid-step and simply stared ahead, his hat still orbiting above him. After what seemed a collection of minutes, a certain startled look appeared across his face. The man briefly looked around, and then hurriedly stretched upward to retrieve his hat. Continuing to look around to see if anyone else had witnessed the event, the man hastened on his way. Sarah and Jason could scarcely maintain their composure until he was out of earshot and they let loose laughing. Sarah, although overjoyed with amusement from the prank, started to become wary of the out-of-place and continuous stream of men in black that kept crossing her path. Jason was also starting to wonder if Sarah's questionable revelation about being stalked by men in black was really, maybe, amid some truth. However, at this point in the relationship, Jason and Sarah didn't talk much about the men in black who kept appearing. They were having too much fun.

As the MIB were identified more and more by both Jason and Sarah, it became increasingly evident that they must constantly be on guard to avoid disclosing that they were in any way responsible for disrupting the law of physics by utilizing Jason's power. Jason and Sarah had both ascertained that the men must be following them in particular and that it must have something to do with Jason's power. Men in black seemed to appear in restaurants, at the movie theater, the grocery store, and even work. They were spotted walking dogs in the park, posing as friendly neighbors collecting their mail, and even agitated rush hour drivers. Perhaps Sarah and Jason should have been more careful with their experiments, not only how much they were discovering, but also how open they had been with parading it publically. But no harm was coming to them and something remained seemingly prankish about the encounters. They were having fun, so the couple decided not to stop now.

There was one such occasion when two boys, about six or seven years old were kicking a soccer ball around in an isolated community field. The field was small and overgrown with patchy leaves and was nestled next to a large pond. Sarah and Jason had decided on a weekend picnic and found a lush area nearby. They had finished their lunch and were watching the youngsters play. One of the boys raised his arms in disappointment when he realized he had kicked the ball too far and it had bounced out into the middle of the pond. The ball slapped the water and floated in the center. The pond was deep and the boys knew if they attempted to swim out and retrieve the ball, they would get in trouble with their mothers not only for getting wet and dirty, but for attempting a dangerous feat.

As the boys stood helpless wondering what to do, Jason walked up, looked at them and said, "Is that your ball?" He pointed to the red kickball rolling atop the rippling pond.

"Yea," one of the boys answered sorrowfully, "but I don't know how we are going to get it." Jason smiled and patted the top of the kid's head. He then stepped softly onto the water without sinking, walked slowly out to the ball with an air of confidence, retrieved it, and then continued his walk back to land. Jason acted as if everything was normal, but he was clearly and effortlessly walking on water. The boys looked both excited and afraid as Jason tossed the ball in their direction.

They were so shocked that they could barely mumble, "thank you." Jason walked away as if nothing out of the ordinary had occurred. Jason walked back to his picnic area and the boys ran off in the distance.

By the time the boys were out of sight, Jason and Sarah had a good laugh over the incident, wondering if the two wide-eyed boys had tried to convince their mothers and friends that they had really witnessed a man walk on water. Their mothers probably tried to inform the boys that only Jesus himself could walk on water and their friends probably thought the boys were either crazy or trying to pull off some sort of prank. It was just the kind of event Jason and Sarah reveled in.

CHAPTER 4

Sarah came out of the grocery store, pushing a jam-packed shopping cart. She was having a lovely day off running errands and preparing to arrange a home-cooked dinner for Jason when her attention was averted. She noticed two men in black standing near her truck, both looking up at the sky.

It was a chilly, windswept September day, cloudless except for one circular cloud which seemed to be the object of the two men's attention. Sarah packed her groceries in the truck, on guard as to what the men were doing, and closed the lid. The men, for several moments now, had not flinched while staring at the lone cloud.

One of the men was middle-aged, tall and lanky with a very waxen pallor. The other man was younger and shorter but also had a thin build. He had dull brown hair and exceptionally rotten teeth for what appeared to be such a young age.

Turning toward them, Sarah boldly drew near and asked, "What do you see?" Both men turned toward her in unison and politely tipped their hats. The tall man's head exposed a sparse, balding crown.

"Just an unusual cloud," he replied, "but I wonder if we might talk to you for a few minutes, Miss Pringle." Sarah immediately furrowed her brow.

The Gray Star Theory

"How do you know my name? And just who are you guys anyway?" Sarah responded with wariness in her demeanor. The older man put up his hands defensively, taking note of her suspicious reaction.

"We mean you no harm. We are observers. Exactly how we know who you are…well, that is one question we cannot answer. My name is Mr. Diamond. My partner here is Mr. Spade." The names gave Sarah the sense that this was some sort of arranged prank, and she quickly returned to her spunky, assertive self.

Detecting a real adventure in the making and not feeling particularly threatened, Sarah replied to Mr. Diamond.

"Alright! If you want to talk, let's get out of the wind and go inside the mall over there where there are some benches to sit comfortably." Sarah pointed in the direction she was referring to, and Mr. Diamond bowed. The two men began to walk while Sarah crept slowly behind them watching their every move and suppressing an involuntary grin. This had to be Jason's work, she imagined. Such good timing, it almost had her alarmed.

Mr. Diamond seemed to be a man in his late fifties who moved with a funny walk. It was almost as if he had suffered some sort of anomaly that he otherwise learned to function usefully. Sarah didn't have the time to ponder why. Her glance fell upon Mr. Spade, who was unusually quiet in the conversation and obviously not the leader of his trade. He did, however, unabashedly display his strikingly discolored smile for the world to perceive. Sarah felt a little sorry for the man who appeared to be her age or perhaps in his early thirties. Unfortunately, she knew that Mr. Spade's unattractive mouth and homely face probably did not work well with the ladies. If he did have difficulties with acceptance of his looks, Mr. Spade certainly did not show it.

Just inside the mall entry were several rows of benches that faced toward each other. The two men took up one bench while Sarah sat across from them in another. They were all seated comfortably, Sarah with her hands folded calmly in her lap while shoppers strolled by, paying them no notice. With a waiting ear, Mr. Diamond began the conversation by saying, "As I mentioned earlier, we are observers.

Our directive is to make no contact, have no interaction, but merely observe. However, we have recently been given the unusual task of contacting you in regard to Mr. Jason Morely. We need to learn how he controls the dark energy. We know that you, Miss Pringle, have an implant in your hand that allows all of your movements to be tracked. We have been using you to observe Mr. Morely. That is about all we can tell you now, but if you help us to understand how Mr. Morely manipulates dark energy, we can give you a story to write that will shock and mystify all mankind. You must not mention our conversation to anyone, especially Mr. Morely, for you may both be in grave danger. We are here to help you."

It was sure a lot of information with an underlying threatening tone, but Sarah showed no fear. She sat quietly for a moment to digest what she had just heard. Something inside her scoffed at the idea that anything Mr. Diamond was telling her was true. She almost found the statement amusing, as if the man had memorized a script from some sort of fantastical movie. Jason must have orchestrated this elaborate hoax. He was probably watching her now, giggling with the notion that she was unsure of what was going on. Sarah did not want to entertain this idea, and instead of looking around for Jason, maintained her composure. She lifted her head assuredly, taking a moment to unite her thoughts.

"You know, Jason is a good friend of mine and I would never do anything to compromise him. Mr. Diamond…if you think I really believe that is your name…tell me…who do you report to?"

With a slight cock of the head, Mr. Diamond replied to her inquiry, "That is a fair question Miss Pringle, but one that we cannot answer now, maybe someday. We certainly don't want you to do or say anything that would adversely affect Mr. Morely. We think you might help us to understand." Mr. Diamond's seemingly monotone voice was beginning to take on a more menacing tone. Undeterred by his vibrato, Sarah answered, "Well, I can't tell you anything because I honestly don't know how he does it." She was being truthful about Jason's power. Mr. Diamond pursed his lips and raised his joined hands to his chest as if praying.

"That is ok. We just require you to watch to see if he does anything different when he negates gravity. Be an observer like us and report back. One of us will be available at all times if you wish to contact us. We must go now, but remember our offer." Mr. Diamond flicked a business card from his black coat pocket into Sarah's direction. She rapidly clutched the card, looking it over from front to back. One side of the card was black with the words AGENT DIAMOND written in white letters. The other side of the card was white and was printed with a phone number in bold, black ink. There was no other information on the card which Sarah found to be foolish and utterly unprofessional. A child could fashion a more creative, informative business card. Sarah looked up quickly with a raised eyebrow, but the men had already gotten up from the bench and left, each going in a different direction. She remained seated on the bench for a while, mulling over what had just been said. She was now unsure what to believe. It seemed too intricate a scenario for Jason to pull off alone, but it was also difficult to believe men in black were real and talking to her. She was particularly intrigued and a little concerned about what Mr. Diamond had said about her having an implant. She fingered the little black spot between her thumb and forefinger and remembered jokingly telling Jason it meant something, but really it had no significant meaning that she knew of. She was also interested by the story the man had offered her to be able to write. What the heck was that all about and what did it mean? Certainly Jason wouldn't offer such a rouse that would belong so close to her heart. Sarah had confided in Jason that she was unhappy in her lack of being able to find a job in the journalism field that she was so passionate and hungry for. Something in her mind was revealing to her that perhaps this was not a joke. Jason played pranks but he wasn't cruel. He knew not to overstep and promise a story that had no truthful bearing.

Shortly after the encounter, Sarah called Jason.

"We need to talk." She felt a surge of urgency to sort out the overload of information swirling in her mind. She fixed dinner at her place with the supplies she had just gotten from the store:

delicious shrimp salad, French bread, and a bottle of champagne. She wanted the date to be romantic and fun like she had first planned, but now its purpose became more about sorting out just who Mr. Diamond and Mr. Spade were, where they came from, and who was responsible for such an elaborate hoax. A couple of hours had passed from the encounter, and after much consideration, Sarah was convinced the meeting was staged. During dinner, she talked about her day, omitting the MIB encounter and playfully forking food into her mouth. What began as a sarcastic and lighthearted dialogue rapidly turned more earnest.

Sarah looked deep into Jason's eyes with seriousness and inquired, "What does it feel like when you, you know, exercise your power?" Taken aback, Jason swallowed hard.

After studying the question for a few minutes he answered, "Pretty much what anyone with a power like that could expect. I have to really concentrate, and when I'm in that zone I can feel a throbbing in my forehead like it is my pulse. It's not intensely strong but definitely noticeable. I know I am getting a little stronger. It must be the practice." Sarah smiled approvingly and continued the discussion intently throughout dinner and dessert. They opened a second bottle of wine and Jason gave Sarah a look as though he had just realized something odd.

"Did you call me over saying we had to talk just to ask me how I feel when I am working my powers?" Sarah laughed heartily.

"No," she responded, "but I am genuinely interested." Jason sipped his wine and licked his lips as a moment of silence passed.

"So? What is it then?" Sarah sighed and then began to narrate the meeting of the two men in black while gauging Jason's expression. It was apparent something was bothering him by the look of concern upon his face.

He put his hands up defensively and muttered, "I swear I had no part in setting that up." Sarah squinted her eyes in an expression of uncertainty. "Honest!" Jason shouted. "Maybe *you* set it up and are acting like you didn't know anything about it to trick me." Sarah scowled with disbelief and poured another glass of wine.

"Please, Jason, I wouldn't stoop that low."

The couple spent a good while continuing to convince each other that neither one of them had set up the MIB encounter. Was it coincidence? Did someone else insert themselves into their playful schemes? Was it true? Both Jason and Sarah ended the night with much on their minds. Jason readied himself to head home and gave Sarah a warm hug and thanked her for the wonderful dinner and entertaining debate. He kissed her on the cheek, threw on his jacket, and got into his car. He waved goodbye as Sarah blew him a kiss from the doorway.

Jason started to drive home, replaying the evening's events in his mind. So deep in thought and feeling a bit tipsy, Jason unintentionally drove through a stop sign without even noticing it. Suddenly, flashing lights of red and blue beamed behind him. He was being pulled over by a patrol car. Jason slowed down and drove to the side of the road where he put his car in the park position. He watched in the rearview mirror as the officer exited his vehicle and approached the left side of Jason's car. The officer used his flashlight to shine into the car window to observe Jason fumbling for his driver's license and insurance papers. The officer stood quietly as Jason, multi-tasking, rolled down the window.

"Good evening, sir," the officer began, "I'm Deputy Cameron. I pulled you over because you failed to stop at a stop sign. I mean, you didn't even slow down, just drove right through it." Jason flashed the policeman a quick, nervous smile. "Have you been drinking, sir?" Deputy Cameron asked. Jason made eye contact with the deputy after handing him his driver's license and insurance.

"No," he answered, but then looked down with admission of surrender. "Well I did have a couple glasses of wine." Deputy Cameron took a step back and examined the driver's license closely.

He immediately ordered, "Please step out of the vehicle, Mr. Morely." The officer was intending to administer a sobriety test, and Jason knew it. Feeling the effects of the wine a little, Jason decided instead of being nervous, he could have some fun. Officer Cameron commanded that Jason exit and walk to the back of the car, facing away from him. Jason, complying, exited the car unflinchingly and stood about four inches off the pavement. Maintaining the distance from foot to ground, Jason began to walk, strolling slowly behind the car as the deputy had directed all the while acting as if everything was completely normal. Officer Cameron was a no-nonsense type of guy who believed in doing everything by the book. He watched Jason's behavior, trying to maintain his composure and not seem alarmed. When Jason was at the location the officer had asked, he flashed him a pleasing grin while still levitating in the air. The officer said nothing and began to cautiously follow the perimeter where Jason had just walked. Deputy Cameron then inspected the area all around Jason's feet, even pulling out a flashlight to make sure there was no funny business going on. The officer knew what he was seeing, but somehow his sensibilities couldn't process it. He continued his examination, becoming more frustrated by the moment, and then finally caved.

"How are you doing that?" Deputy Cameron was scratching his head. Jason shrugged his shoulders and answered, "Do what?" The officer didn't respond but walked hurriedly back to his patrol car thinking he should call this in. Something seemed off and suspicious. Just then, a second patrol car pulled in behind him. Deputy Cameron quickly ordered Jason to put his hands behind his back and detained him with handcuffs. Jason complied. The second officer exited his vehicle and began to walk toward them.

"Stay here." Deputy Cameron instructed toward Jason, looking back down at his feet to make sure Jason was still levitating. He turned and ran over to the second officer, Deputy Hastings. Jason delicately lowered his feet to the ground, hands behind his back and his head forward with a serious look upon his face.

Deputy Cameron shouted, "Come take a look at this guy. You won't believe it!"

Deputy Hastings, a greying veteran, immediately inquired as to the situation.

"Is he high?" asked the approaching deputy. Deputy Cameron smirked.

"High? I guess you can say he's a little high. He doesn't touch the ground. Literally, he is standing on air. I can't believe it myself. I can't believe I'm saying it out loud." By this time, Jason had fully composed himself and appeared perfectly sober. As the two officers advanced toward him with caution, Deputy Cameron was shocked to notice that Jason was no longer levitating.

With a stammer in his voice, Deputy Cameron queried "Please show my friend here what you just did." Jason looked bewildered and could only generate an unknowing shrug. After a minute of embarrassing silence, the first officer began to realize he had been had. The second officer called Cameron aside and they whispered for a minute. Jason chuckled lightly.

The police officers then returned to face Jason, Deputy Cameron saying, "I'm just going to give you a warning this time. Watch those stop signs." As Deputy Hastings walked away, Jason gave the other officer a knowing wink.

CHAPTER 5

Sarah's mother, Nadine, was a firm, fastidious woman about fifty years old and very class conscious. She always dressed flawlessly, and as a real estate agent, preferred to deal with upper income clientele. She had always encouraged Sarah to only date men who could afford her preferred status and lifestyle. She wanted what was best for Sarah and was sure that social status and money would be the winning ticket.

Sarah and Jason had been in a serious relationship now for over a month, and although they were taking it slow and had not yet moved in together, they were constant companions in their free time. It was now the time when mother was coming to visit, and she indeed wanted to meet the man her beloved daughter had been boasting about. Sarah had referred to Jason frequently in conversation when talking to her mother, but really hadn't revealed anything about him.

Sarah met her mother at the airport, procuring a stretch limousine to escort them in, as Nadine wouldn't have it any other way. It had been almost a year since mother and daughter had seen each other face to face due to the distance between them. Sarah adored her mother, but did not feel the same about marriage and money equating to happiness the same way her mother had always driven into her. Sarah was an only child, and therefore an overly protected, overly adored one. As they drove to Nadine's hotel, Sarah was met with a barrage of questions about Jason and his career prospects. Suffice it to say, Sarah assured her mother that Jason was very talented but also reminded her that they were merely dating, just friends. Sarah was thankful her mother had chosen to stay in a five-star hotel this year rather than invade her small, cramped home which she knew her mother loathed. Nadine urged her daughter to meet her for dinner accompanied by Jason so she could meet him for herself. Sarah agreed to bring Jason to the hotel. The meeting had to happen sometime, and hopefully her mother would find the same unique something in him that Sarah had instantly been drawn to.

By this time, Jason had evolved somewhat since meeting Sarah. He now relished the opportunity to discretely have fun with people using his "talent." Sarah also enjoyed this little game and had learned how to play along, oftentimes by pretending not to see the obvious. She also knew it lent to the confidence Jason so desperately needed. It was good for both body and mind. When they had their moments of fun, they would later relive the episodes and share many laughs. It allowed for their relationship to flourish.

To properly meet Nadine for dinner, the couple dressed for the first time as if they were about to meet the Queen of England. Sarah glided elegantly in an over-the-top, eggplant purple dress and Jason, reserved and demure, appeared handsomely dapper in his gray tuxedo. The couple met Nadine in the lobby of her hotel and proceeded to the lavish dining room, aptly named *The Palace*. They entered a white room that was chandeliered in sparkling crystal and adorned in fine china. A waiter pulled out the chair for Nadine, who didn't notice immediately that when she was seated, her chair was about an inch above the floor. It was obviously Jason's doing, and one that helped to ease his growing anxiety. He knew women like Nadine, no matter where their intentions lied, never found him to be the archetype worthy of love. After everyone was seated, the conversation began at Nadine's behest. Sarah's mother, after immediately asking Jason about his work and future plans, started spouting loudly about her own successes in real estate. She bragged about the 2.5 million dollar property she just opened escrow on as well as other endeavors she felt were of significant accolades. In her boring reverie, Jason felt delight being able to be in control over her. For ten minutes now, Nadine's chair had steadily suspended itself in the air. It took Jason a great deal of energy to maintain, but the fun outweighed the exertion. Now, Jason could barely contain his longing to cease her overbearing exchange. He allowed her chair to fall to the floor with a noticeable and audible thud. Nadine gasped, but quickly pretended as if everything was how it should be. Sarah kicked Jason under the table, unappreciative of how he had just treated her mother. Nadine was obviously flustered, but she used every ounce of composure within her to remain a polite and collective figure. One inch from air suspension to floor does not seem like much, but it sure gave Nadine a start. Her first thought was that the chair had broken under her weight. Sarah continued to give Jason a knowing frown, but he was able to appear concerned as though the event was an innocent fluke.

They finished dinner without further incident, continuing the conversation the way Nadine desired. The trio feasted upon fois gras, escargot, red wine, and other fine dishes with French names Jason had no clue how to pronounce. He tried to act as friendly and sophisticated as he could, but knew his impression upon Sarah's mother was dreadfully underwhelming. As a gentleman, he paid the bill without even so much as a thank you from Nadine, and Jason couldn't understand how such a wonderfully gentle, kind, and down-to-earth person like Sarah could be the product of such a prideful, entitled woman.

As they left the restaurant, Sarah couldn't help but notice a MIB loitering in the lobby that looked very similar to one she had observed at the airport. It seemed she was the only one to notice. Jason sulked behind mother and daughter as they walked and Nadine was unaware of the men in black at all.

Nadine took her daughter by the arm, interlacing her bejeweled hand, and asked with an affably forced tone in Jason's direction, "Mr. Morely, would you mind waiting here in the lobby while my daughter escorts me to my room? I just want a moment to speak with her privately." Jason bowed with his hand outstretched, a gesture to show that he had no objection. Without so much as a parting goodbye, Nadine turned with her daughter in tow and strode toward an elevator.

After a shared moment of silence inside the elevator, Nadine began, "My daughter, how I love you, sweet darling." She started to unwrap the fur scarf from her neck as the elevator began to rise. Sarah couldn't tell if her mother was being sincere or if this was the prelude to a disapproving lecture. She stood silently, waiting to take in the barrage of emotions she knew her mother was intending to unleash.

"I hate to be so frank," Nadine huffed, "but seriously Sarah, this guy seems like a dud. Why don't you come to the city and I'll set you up with some of the well-to-do young men." She caressed her daughter's face, but Sarah, looking away at first, backed away from Nadine entirely and flashed an annoyed glance. "You don't even know him, mother."

Nadine smiled and stepped off the elevator. Nadine's high heels clicked across the marble tiled hallway as she made her way toward her room.

"You always do this!" Sarah exclaimed as she followed behind her, "You don't think any man is good for me…I've made up my mind though. I don't care what you or anyone else thinks. I know Jason is special." Nadine, who was just about to clasp the door handle to her room, immediately perked up and gave her daughter an exasperated look.

"Honestly, Sarah! You should value my opinion. I have experience in these matters. You are my only child and I only want what is best for you." Sarah hung her head.

"I know you do, mother, but what I think is best for me might not be what you think is best." A pause elapsed, and then Nadine finally entered her hotel room and sat down properly upon one of the dining room chairs adjacent to the door. She snapped a finger, and with her back toward Sarah, ordered her to pour a glass of chardonnay. Sarah obliged.

"Give Jason a chance, mother. Get to know him. Learn about him. Maybe you will see what I see. Please, mother, I beg you." Sarah began to manually open a chilled bottle of wine. She wiped off a crystal wine glass and dispensed the costly liquid. Nadine was not impressed with Sarah's plea, so therefore did not respond.

Placing the wine glass with a clink in front of her mother, Sarah announced, "Love you, mother. I've got to go. It's been great seeing you." She kissed her mother on the forehead before hastily exiting the room.

Once she was several feet down the hall, Sarah sighed a breath of relief. She was distressed that she had to leave her mother so suddenly, but she just couldn't take it when her mom acted this way. She always loved and cared about her mother, but Sarah was well aware that unless she found a millionaire man with a socially elite family, he would never be good enough for Nadine. Sarah was the only child of her mother, Nadine and father, Elliott who died when she was young.

As Sarah began the descent in the elevator back to the lobby where Jason had been waiting, there was a detour to another floor where the elevator stopped to collect more passengers. When the doors opened to the second floor, Sarah was stunned to see a lurching man, dressed in a black suit, step inside. He stood motionless while the elevator traveled at what seemed to be an eternity. Sarah did not acknowledge the man, but she did, however, take mental notes of what he looked like. She was beginning to wonder if the men in black that kept reappearing everywhere she went were different people or the same man in disguise. Was it Mr. Diamond? This man wore a black top hat and had a thick brown beard and moustache. He appeared to be middle-aged with a resemblance to Abraham Lincoln. Sarah decided she would start writing down and sketching the MIB appearances as they occurred and how they had already transpired to see if there was a pattern. She was certain these encounters would not be ending anytime soon, which is why she was also beginning to have a sinking feeling that the MIB were not a hoax but a real entity. What she couldn't understand was what they wanted with her. It's not like Jason's powers were harming anyone or interfering with anything. It was just a rare skill that allowed him to levitate and accomplish other small feats.

When the elevator doors opened to the lobby, Sarah rushed out first in a half-jog toward Jason, who was standing in exactly the same place she had left him. She grabbed his hand and pointed over in the direction of the elevator so Jason could get a glimpse of the man in black, but it was one second too late. The doors had just finished closing when Jason's attention was focused toward the departing elevator. Sarah, trying to keep a cool demeanor, urged Jason out the door to a taxi where she whispered her experience with the man in the elevator in short, choppy sentences. The discussion was focused mainly on if the men in black were real or who could possibly be the perpetrator of such a scheme. Since they had traveled close to two hundred miles from city to city to visit Nadine at a halfway point from where she lived, it seemed out of the way, difficult to carry out, and costly to continue a rouse from such a distance. However, Jason and Sarah were still not sure of the situation nor the reality of Jason's power to believe it could be anything other than a well-planned hoax.

The taxi ride home was filled with an unusual silence. Part of it was because Jason knew Sarah's mother had not liked him and probably had said terrible things about him. He was hopeful that Sarah had defended him against any animosity her mother may have held against him, but he wasn't certain. He also wasn't sure if Sarah was upset with the fact he had used his power to entertain himself at the expense of Nadine and her striking snobbery. He figured, however, with how much Sarah had grown to know his personality that he had only done the trickery out of social anxiety as a tool to ease his involuntary angst. The other part of the silence was due to the recurring sightings of the men in black. They seemed to be getting closer and more involved. If they were real, what did they want? The questions and unknowing of what was really going on made both Jason and Sarah feel excruciatingly out of control. Jason began to feel a twinge of anger bubble up inside him. He wanted to do the right thing and to fight for justice. What was right and just, however, was a complete mystery, and something Jason could not fathom. He decided the only way to achieve any sort of relief from the turmoil that was currently transpiring in his life was to learn more about his power and control it for worthwhile purposes.

"I love you," he uttered quietly in the back seat of the cab. Sarah's eyes opened widely, and she smiled a short but delighted grin. "I want you to know that whatever happens, who I become, and no matter what the forces of this world desire, that you are the only real love I have ever known."

Sarah remained silent as Jason expressed himself. They both knew their relationship was still relatively new, but the growth and understanding of each other within it had been exponentially greater than that of many enduring marriages. Sarah didn't have to say it back. Jason already knew. Sarah no longer had command over her feelings despite what her mother felt or Jason believed. It was inevitable, a force of nature.

Hours later, the taxi slowly swayed up the cracked driveway of Sarah's home and dropped them off. As she sauntered up the path, Jason stood quietly in the street. He paid the fare and thanked the driver. When Sarah neared the front door, she stopped when she heard a strange noise. She glanced at the doorknob and keyhole, stunned that the metal was rapidly moving back and forth, almost vibrating. She froze in absolute fear. After a few seconds, the door opened slightly, about two inches, and gently creaked as it slowly widened. Sarah backed away quietly, then ran to Jason. It was the first time he had seen her truly afraid.

"It's okay. It's me!" he told her, grasping her shoulders then pulling her in tightly for a reassuring hug. "I wanted to see if I could do something different. I can levitate myself and others. I can move objects a bit. Now I know I can break in anywhere I want. I can pick a lock and open a door." Sarah's eyes looked up to his and she breathed with an incredible sigh.

"I was really scared," she moaned, "I thought it was an intruder!" Jason chuckled lightly and escorted her to the door, rubbing her back in consolation.

"I'm sorry. I should have warned you. I didn't really know what I could do or what would happen. I never want to scare you, Sarah." She smiled as she put her purse on the kitchen table and slumped in an oversized chair in the living room.

"I know. I trust you."

CHAPTER 6

Sarah entered work feeling cheerful and bright. The last couple of days had proved uneventful, and she believed she and Jason were finally becoming free of the chaos both her mother and the men in black had been creating. Around two o'clock in the afternoon, Sarah had left her receptionist's desk to prepare a meeting room for one of the company's senior advisors. He had requested the one and only meeting room in the entire building that was concealed from external view, not the typical glass windowed rooms and offices the rest of the building boasted. She had only been inside the room a minute when she heard the door burst open, and two people walked inside.

It was two men, and Sarah instantly recognized both.

"How can I help you, Mr. Diamond, Mr. Spade?" There was a rush of palpable sarcasm and annoyance in her voice. The men seemed undeterred by her demeanor.

"Greetings, Miss Pringle," Mr. Diamond responded while standing at attention. Sarah stopped his speech immediately by holding up her hand. He had no intention of approaching her, but it was obvious by her body language that she was troubled nonetheless.

"Don't come any closer, and listen up." The two men stood with their sunglasses and hats still on, their tailored suits black against the stark white office walls with their hands folded behind their backs. They almost appeared militant in their conduct and remained impassive. Sarah continued with a hostility and firmness in her voice.

"I don't know who put you up to this or what you think you are doing continuing this ridiculous charade, but I am sick of it. You and your little cohorts are popping up in my life way too often and you are starting to get too personal. Now I like a good joke, believe me, but if I see you guys one more time I will contact the police. I will get a restraining order against you for stalking me and I will also not tolerate you coming into the lives of my family and friends. So I suggest you get the hell out of here and my life." The seriousness in Sarah's tone surprised even her, but once again, the men were unwavering. Sara hallowed Mr. Diamond to respond to her demand.

"Miss Pringle, I beg of you to please understand, this is not a joke. We mean you no harm and do not want to do anything to upset you. Our only desire is to observe and learn of the power Mr. Morely possesses. Has his power changed at all recently? Please tell us what you know. We believe him to be quite special." Sarah was so upset that her hands balled into fists. Inadvertent tears filled her eyes.

"I swear that if I see you again I am calling the cops. Get out of here! I'm sick of this stupid game. Leave!" She turned her back to the men and shielded her face from them, hoping they wouldn't see her cry. Mr. Diamond, unabashed, had one final statement before departing.

"You will be sorry that you are making this harder than it has to be." Sarah didn't move. She waited for the door to close behind her before she held her breath and gathered herself with as much positivity she could muster before finishing the meeting room setup. She decided she was not going to let some jokesters ruin her day.

At this point in Jason and Sarah's relationship, they were beginning to have dinner almost nightly and most times even spending the night at one or the other's home. Tonight was no different. It was a cold day with light snow, and Jason decided he would be the one to cook tonight. As he stirred a large pot of soup, Sarah noticed that Jason seemed out of sorts. She decided to ignore it and continue the night without further commotion, but Jason was the one who could no longer keep to himself. He let the soup simmer and poured Sarah a well-deserved glass of wine. She instantly brought it to her lips and sipped with delight.

The taste, however, soured when Jason explained, "Those men you talked about, Mr. Diamond and Mr. Spade...They paid me a visit today." Sarah's forehead scrunched in anger as she rose from her chair.

"What time was this?" Jason thought for a moment as he recounted his day.

"Around four o'clock I would say. I was close to getting off work." Sarah approached Jason and put her hands firmly on his face as if to acquire his undivided attention.

"I'm done with this. I don't know who is doing this but it's not funny anymore. I'm getting angry." Jason sighed and laid his warm hand upon hers that were still clinging to his jaw.

"I know what you mean," he sympathized. "I just can't figure it out though. Whoever set this up, obviously not you or me, has to know that we don't find it funny anymore. I just don't know of anybody that would want to do this. I don't have many friends or family. Do you have any ideas?" Sarah shook her head sadly.

"I can't figure it out either. They came to me today too, but earlier in the day. I warned them to stay away and they didn't." Sarah hesitated, rummaging her mind for the next move. "I am calling the cops!" In a huff of anger, Sarah set her wine glass firmly on the kitchen counter and walked towards the telephone. Jason hastily departed after her, taking her hand again.

"Please, sweetheart. This will have to end eventually. Let's just have a nice night together."

Sarah pondered the idea for a moment and drew closer to him, planting a delicate kiss on his lips. Jason advised that they spend the rest of the night omitting any discussion or worry over Mr. Diamond, Mr. Spade, or any men in black. Instead, the couple enjoyed a wonderfully cooked dinner while Jason divulged to Sarah that earlier in the day he had started a fire atop the gas-fueled stovetop using his powers. He compared himself sardonically as a "jedi master" and that soon he would be able to read minds and control people's thoughts and actions. As he relished the ideas his head began to fill with, Sarah quietly questioned how powerful Jason really was.

CHAPTER 7

After work the following day, Jason flung the door open to Sarah's home where she sat peacefully reading a book. She instantly panicked when she saw the distressed look on Jason's face. They stared momentarily in silence until Jason began to recount his experience with a jolted stammer in his voice.

"Those men, you know, Mr. Diamond and his stupid sidekick. They…" Jason didn't want to alarm Sarah, but he knew he had no other choice but to tell her the truth for her own protection.

"What?" Sarah pleaded with a quiver of rage.

"They attacked me," Jason began, "first Mr. Diamond was talking, like saying all kinds of stuff I didn't understand. He was talking really fast and when I gave him a little laugh, he threatened me. He was saying all this crazy stuff about my powers. I think the guy is mentally unhinged." Sarah grimaced while jumping to her feet.

"That bastard! We have to do something."

Jason urged Sarah to sit down and delicately explained, "I know you're scared and I don't have the answer as to who is doing this or why or what the hell Mr. Diamond wants from us, but if we go to the cops, they're not going to believe us." A tear trailed from Sarah's eye as a sense of hopelessness passed through her. She then released Jason's hand she had been firmly holding and composed herself, revealing the strong woman she had always been.

"What did he do to you? What did he say?" Sarah remained calm as Jason attempted to put the facts of the events gently.

"Mr. Diamond was saying the power I have is something only I have and that it is an extraterrestrial cosmic force that no human should have ever acquired or learned to use. I'm some sort of anomaly I guess, and there are no others like me…I'm like an X-Men…" Jason chuckled but Sarah did not find the joke funny. She raised her eyebrows insistently, a sign for Jason to continue the story. "That's what I told them. I told them I was an X-Men and laughed about it. Then, Mr. Diamond grabbed my arm and twisted it, trying to pull it behind my back. I saw Mr. Spade with handcuffs and a knife. I just pulled my hands free from him and ran. Now I'm here."

The men had not attempted to chase after Jason when he escaped, but the couple definitively established that there was definitely something sinister about Mr. Diamond and Mr. Spade. They also realized the men were becoming more brazen and that they knew Jason and Sarah would not be able to go to the cops for help. It would make them look like lunatics. The couple decided that while they tried to figure out what was going on, they would take vacation time off from work and head to Nadine's to hide out in her private estate where they would most likely be the safest. Perhaps the distance and promptness would deter any more men in black from stalking them, especially Mr. Diamond and Mr. Spade.

Jason decided to rent a car, an inconspicuous, white Ford truck. He picked up Sarah from her house the next morning after she promptly packed her bags. Jason escorted Sarah the five hundred miles to Nadine's residence, trying desperately to make the drive seem like a fun road trip rather than running away. However, instead of the spunk and happiness they would have otherwise experienced on a short road trip, like singing wildly to rock 'n' roll classics and playing fun trivia games, Jason and Sarah discussed possibilities and answers to questions. The more they questioned, the more confused and despondent they became. Since the only apparent reason for the encounters was Jason's power, the two began pondering deeper into his talent.

"Even if I was the only person who had this power," Jason started, "Don't you think it's pretty lame? I mean, it's not like I can do anything that someone would want to harm me for. I guess I can pick locks though, so maybe Mr. Diamond wants me to be a robber or something. I can work for the dark side." Jason and Sarah both had a giggle, but quickly resumed their speculation. Several minutes of silence passed when Jason stated somberly, "My power is not special. Sure I can make people levitate and manipulate objects, but they are acting like I hold the fate of humanity in my hands. My power is nothing to kill over."

Sarah interjected and stated, "You don't know that…The only thing this could mean, if it really is real, is that you haven't yet unlocked the true potential of your power and that it is something more profound than we know."

Jason looked doubtful and confessed, "I took time off of work to figure this out. I don't think this is anything extreme. The fate of the world is not mine to conquer. I haven't unlocked some part of the brain people want to conduct science experiments on. I'm an ordinary guy with a talent that doesn't do anything to people except give me some excitement to see the wonder in their eyes." Again, Sarah interjected, this time with more fervor.

"What if you did use it for evil? Maybe they want to learn how to get your power for themselves and hurt people. Maybe they want to change you and make you into like a mind-controlled super-alien-robot-assassin." Jason could not control the hearty laugh that overcame him upon hearing Sarah's theory. In fact, he could barely hold onto the steering wheel. Sarah joined in, but still remained heavy-hearted.

Jason gasped from laughing so hard, then declared, "You shouldn't be a journalist, Sarah. You should definitely be a sci-fi author. You could name your book *Super Alien Robot Assassin*. It would surely be a bestseller!" Sarah smirked and finally felt a sense of safety as they drove the rest of the way to her mother's house.

The Gray Star Theory

Sarah had only been to her mother's new home once. It was an over-the-top lavish house with six rooms, large yard, and exquisite amenities like a wrapping veranda, swimming pool, garden, and water features. The property was gated and the only entrance and exit was manned by a guard at all times. Sarah's mother was by no means the crème-de-la-crème of wealth, but she had enough to budget the luxuries she felt her life deserved. Nadine was thankful for two things: having only one child and benefitting financially upon the death of Sarah's father. Nadine wasn't a cold human being. She had been devoted to her husband, loved him dearly, and doted on her young daughter up until the time Sarah decided to become an adult and branch out on her own. Nadine's obsession with luxury and grandeur occurred later in life when she felt compelled to fill the void the death of her husband and independence of her daughter left. She joined women's organizations and went on lavish shopping sprees, traveling around the world until she finally felt fulfilled enough to get a job for the first time in her life. Nadine was able to get her real estate license and began selling expensive homes. Her love for all things rich and expensive continued to blossom and eventually became ingrained into her soul.

As Jason and Sarah entered the wrought iron gate leading into the grand estate, Nadine walked out gracefully onto the pillared entryway of the house with a beaming smile on her face. She was impeccably dressed as if she was expecting the arrival of the Pope, and her demeanor was equally proper. Jason and Sarah ascended the wide staircase to the front door where Nadine instantly spread her arms and embraced her daughter warmly. She kissed Sarah's cheek and gazed into her eyes as if she hadn't seen her in years. All the while, she completely ignored Jason whom Nadine was only allowing to stay in her home because of her daughter's eager beseeching.

A hanging plant that decorated the front terrace, not far from where they were standing while Sarah and Nadine exchanged greetings, instantly fell to the ground, interrupting the reception.

Broken gladiola stems, petals, and leaves lay somberly against the now dirt covered white wood.

"I'll help you with that," Jason exclaimed. He quickly bent down to lend a hand in cleaning the mess, hoping he had used the power for Nadine to finally give him some acknowledgement. Nadine gestured him away and placed her other hand against her fluttering heart.

"What in the world…" Sarah gave Jason a knowing signal that was laced with displeasure. "Let's just go inside, mother. We will clean this up later." Sarah and Nadine walked past the crouching Jason who was shoveling the mess with his hands into a pile. Without finishing the task, he stood up, brushed off his hands, and followed the women.

Once inside the front door, both Jason and Sarah were met with a breathtaking sight. A double grand staircase fashioned in dark, glossy wood stood out against the white and silver marble floor just past the artistically decorated foyer. Jason's jaw dropped at the sight of such luxury. Nadine quickly took Sarah by the hand and led her away as Jason, still inspecting the entirety of the massive vestibule, began to arrange for the luggage he knew he would be toting inside.

Nadine led her daughter through the kitchen and into a small office, or more like a relaxing powder room some would say, and sat her daughter firmly upon a velvet-covered, tasseled day bed. Nadine began to speak while looking her daughter in the eye with an expression of dread.

"What is going on, my darling? Are you in danger? Is it that man? Are the police after you? Are you involved in something illegal?" Nadine was practically shaking Sarah's shoulders in a frenzy of distress. Sarah calmly took her mother's hands and guided her to sit by her side.

"No mother. It's nothing like that. We just wanted to get away from the hectic work and chaos of the city." Nadine squinted her eyes in disbelief.

"You traded one city for another, my dear. Vacations are usually spent on a beach with cocktails fashioned from exotic fruits. People also don't usually opt to vacation at their mother's house. So tell me, my dearest daughter, what is the matter?" Sarah giggled at the way her mother put it.

"Believe it or not, I love to vacation at my mother's. This will be a good time for you to get to know Jason better, and we just want to have some time away from the ravaging mediocrity of everyday life. It's only a week or so, mother. We will be out of your hair in no time." Sarah stood calmly and kissed her mother on the forehead. A moment of silence passed as both stood to exit back toward the foyer when Nadine quickly stopped and spun Sarah around.

"I know what this is," she began with a note of discouragement in her voice, "you want to be serious with him. You want me to get to know him and approve of him."

Sarah was not amused and responded with a distraught defense, "No, mother, that is not it at all…and his name is Jason. I was simply suggesting that we don't get to see each other all that often so you might as well take the time to get to know him before you assume he is a complete loser." Sarah ended the conversation, annoyed with the haughty conduct her mother always flaunted. Both women went out to find Jason who was heaving large suitcases into two adjoining guest rooms on the ground floor. Sarah aided Jason with the undertaking while Nadine went to prepare a cocktail.

After getting settled in, the trio sat down to a nicely prepared dinner. Everything was going smoothly; even Nadine was talking with Jason as if she was thoroughly entertained with the conversation, until it was time for her to ready herself for bed. The fastidious woman had a strict beauty regimen that took her about an hour to perform before actually falling asleep. The timing was perfect because Sarah figured that now with their bellies full and her mother readying for bed, the couple could investigate their situation a little more meticulously instead of just speculating the real reason for their unplanned visit.

Jason and Sarah entered an office workspace on the ground floor and closed the door for privacy. Sarah flicked on the computer and began to do some research on the internet. Distracted, Jason paced around the room while examining the beautiful pieces of artwork on the walls and the leather-bound books set upon dustless, grand oak cases. He could only focus on Nadine and not the situation at hand.

"I can't get your mother to like me." Jason sighed with dissatisfaction.

Sarah wasn't listening much, but quietly replied, "Yeah, don't feel bad. She's like this with everyone." Jason continued to pace, making statements aloud that Sarah unintentionally ignored. She researched for about half an hour, eyes fixed steadily on the computer screen, before finding an article that seemed both credible and elaborate.

"Jason, sit down, you have to hear this." Jason complied and sat upon a leather setee with a quilted pattern upholstery. He tried to find a relaxing position, but found himself twisting and turning until Sarah's voice arose after a long, uninterrupted pause. She began to read the article that she had now been fixed upon aloud:

"It has been widely questioned as to whether the men in black organization exists. Some believe the organization is rather small, consisting of either a small number of government officials assembled to keep evidence of UFO's and extraterrestrials out of the public knowledge or consisting of alien beings themselves with the ability to appear in human form. The men in black have a certain appearance to them. Many believe they are tall and alien-like with no eyebrows, eyelashes, facial hair or head hair. They have been described to be men that are extremely pale in complexion with almost translucent skin and can give a feeling of anxiety and fear to the person whom they encounter. The men dress in dark business suit attire typically accompanied by black ties, hats, sunglasses, briefcases, and/or walking canes. It is believed that if in fact the men in black are real, they have only revealed themselves to a small number of reported victims. The purpose for their visits is to quell a person from researching or speaking out publicly about UFO and extraterrestrial sightings or experiences. The aim for the men in black is to keep any information about UFOs or extraterrestrial life forms secretive and under speculative scrutiny. Reports of men in black encounters have varied from the men posing as government officials, military men, or salesman. Sometimes the men in black appear singly and other times in pairs or trios. Most reported encounters have left a mark of terror and worry on the people who have been confronted by them, some to the extent of madness and life-long fear."

Jason and Sarah looked at each other questioningly with a bout of astonishment and confusion upon their stare.

"This makes no sense," Jason began, "we aren't involved in any UFO or extraterrestrial stuff, and I know you don't really have a tracker implanted in your hand." He chuckled slightly at the thought of Sarah believing that he believed her.

Sarah rolled her eyes and replied, "it can't be me, it's obvious it has something to do with your power since that is what Mr. Diamond and Mr. Spade were interested in knowing about. It's the only thing they kept asking me. They wanted me to observe your powers."

Jason was intrigued by the article, but still acting playful, he joked, "Do you think my power can connect me to aliens or summon UFOs?" Sarah nudged a laughing Jason with her elbow. "It has to do with something we apparently don't know or understand. Look at us right now. We took a vacation and time away from work not to visit my mom but to hide out from men in black who are stalking and terrorizing us for no reason we know of other than you can make people and objects levitate and open doors and stuff."

Jason though a moment and confessed, "These men in black act as if I can read people's minds or control their brains or contact aliens or something." The notion made Jason edge a smile from the corner of his mouth. In wonderment he replied, "maybe I can."

Sarah, the most encouraging of all people toward the use of Jason's power responded, "Maybe you *can* read minds, control people, rule the world…whatever you might be able to do, it's just a theory. From what we know, you can't seem to do anything harmful and that's what I was trying to tell Mr. Diamond. They didn't listen. So now we have to figure out how to get rid of them." Jason started to yawn as if the stalking and attempted assault were a joke.

"How do you propose I do that?" Jason asked when the yawn subsided.

Sarah stared him in the eye with the answer that seemed obvious, "stop using your power—at least until we figure out how to get rid of the men in black. If they will go this far as to blatantly attempt to harm you in broad daylight then they might go as far as to kill you. So it's not funny anymore, okay Jason? We need to be serious. I would be lost without you and I don't want anything bad to happen." The delicacy of Sarah's voice as she spoke the final sentence made Jason's heart leap. He leaned in to kiss her, first giving her a glance of understanding. He then took her by the hand and led Sarah to her room.

"We will research this more later. Just rest for right now, and don't worry." She sighed with relief and hoped she would be able to rest peacefully.

CHAPTER 8

Sarah's nerves continued to quiver the next morning as she sleepily walked into the kitchen to get a cup of coffee. Jason was still soundly asleep in an adjacent room, but Nadine, an early riser, was already deep into scones and marmalade, coffee, and a newspaper. She greeted her daughter and began to announce the plans she had made for the three of them that day. Sarah cut her mother off almost immediately.

"I just want to stay in today, mother. I'm actually not feeling so great." A look of worry crossed Nadine's face and she set down her newspaper and reached over to feel her daughter's forehead.

"My poor baby, let me see if you have a fever." Jason must have heard the conversation in the kitchen close by and woken up. He entered the room, still dressed in his pajamas and interjected, "You probably don't feel well because you didn't sleep well last night. You were having terrible nightmares. You were shouting so loudly I could hear you in the next room. Are you okay?"

Sarah nodded her head, "I'm fine. I just need to relax. I think I'm just overly stressed." Nadine, disappointed by the thought of her daughter staying in all day, agreed that Sarah needed to relax and offered to draw her a de-stressing bubble bath. Sarah kindly declined, so Nadine decided to let Sarah do what she wanted and made her own plans to go out. After drinking some coffee and chatting about their sleep, Sarah walked back into the office where she sat down at the computer and began researching men in black again.

Jason was beginning to think Sarah might be going crazy. The men in black had been a non-stop obsession now for the last few days, much more so than usual. He could understand her worry though. Both had felt threatened and terrorized by the men in black they had encountered, but there was still something unreal about the whole event. Even with the evidence blatantly continuing to appear in their faces, Jason still could not get his mind to cooperate that a men in black organization actually existed.

Amidst the silent air while Sarah researched and Jason stood nearby, the telephone rang loudly. Nadine raced down the stairs and picked it up on the third ring.

"Hello?" She concentrated as she heard static at the other end. "Hello!" she uttered again, this time a little louder. Sarah and Jason entered into the foyer where Nadine was standing. She hardly noticed as she was focusing on the noises emitting from the telephone. Static continued, but then a man's voice began to speak. His voice sounded garbled and robotic as if he were in an area with terrible reception.

"I can't understand you, sir." Nadine continued the phrases over and over again before finally hanging up. She then looked over at Sarah and Jason. "That was odd. It sounded like a man asking to speak with Mr. Morely concerning an accident," Nadine expressed in a questioning tone, "I couldn't understand his name or what he was referring to though. I tried my best."

Sarah, who had been leaning wearily against the wall, quickly sprung to her feet, resting her hands firmly on a nearby table. "No one knows we are here. Who could possibly know Jason Morely is here except me and you, mother?" Nadine raised her shoulders to gesture that she did not know.

"My darling, I may have heard wrong. I don't know for sure they were asking for Mr. Morely. It sounded something like that but it was probably a wrong number call. The reception was terrible and the man sounded as if he was a million miles away." Sarah interjected, turning to Jason, "if he was talking about you, Jason, what would he mean by accident?" Jason shrugged with a half-hearted smile.

"Beats me!" Sarah began to ponder all the things Jason had told her about his childhood and adolescence, trying to recall if he had ever been injured or involved in a traumatic experience that others would constitute as an accident. Nothing popped out at her. Perhaps it really was a wrong number call, but something else told Sarah in her gut that it was someone looking for them, someone more sinister.

Interrupting the long pause in conversation, Nadine asked, "What is going on with you two? You are so jumpy and worried, my darling. Your minds seem to be occupied in deep thought. If you are in some sort of trouble you should tell me so I can help." Sarah and Jason glanced at each other and quickly agreed to tell Nadine everything they had been experiencing. Most parents would never believe such a wild story as what Jason and Sarah were currently entrenched, but Nadine knew her daughter inside and out. She knew Sarah was not playing a joke and legitimately felt fear and chaos welling up into her life more and more with each passing hour. However, Nadine's reaction was like any pragmatist or skeptic would be: unbelievable. There had to be some rational explanation.

"Sarah, darling, if Jason really does have powers, tell him to tell me what I'm thinking about right now."

Sarah smirked and replied, "It doesn't work like that. He only knows how to do certain things and mind reading isn't one of them."

Nadine stood in place with her hands on her hips and demanded, "Show me what you can do, Jason. Anything. Just prove to me you have these so-called powers so I can see it and believe it for myself." Jason began to concentrate before Sarah stopped him.

"Mother! We are not making this up. It's not a joke. This is real and it's getting serious. If you want to help us, just keep us inside this house until we figure out some sort of plan." Sarah had become visibly annoyed, so Nadine remained quiet and left the room so the couple could discuss the matter without being disturbed any further. Because of the circumstances, Nadine was still unsure of what to think. Sarah thought it would be best to do some more research, so the couple returned to the office once more.

"If we are going to figure this out we need to go over the possibilities, Sarah. We can learn everything there is to know about men in black online, but we can't know why unless we figure it out ourselves." Sarah looked over her shoulder at Jason and nodded her head in agreement. She turned off the computer and sat next to him with her hands cupping her cheeks in discouragement.

"I can't even begin to think of why this is happening. I know it involves your power. That's what the men in black talked about wanting me to observe. Your powers must be more unique than we realized." Sarah thought a moment while Jason agreed.

He then asked, "Don't you think the only way to know the true potential of my power is to experiment with it? We can only unlock the mystery that way I suppose."

Sarah hung her head in worry and replied, "I think that's a bad idea. Your power may be harmful or cause you to do something that can't be undone. I think what we have been doing was okay but we don't want to find out if you can do something horrible. Besides, they probably can track us when you use your power and that's how they have been able to stalk us and find us." Jason perked instantly when he realizing he had only used his power once since arriving at Nadine's house.

"It could be, but they have stalked you and confronted you when I wasn't around. Maybe the power is what started it all and they have been following us ever since. There's no telling when they might find us, but…"

Jason and Sarah froze in their tracks when they heard a loud, repetitious knock at the door. Jason emerged silently, peeking cautiously through the peep hole with Sarah close behind. Jason saw a little old man standing at the door. He looked harmless, but most importantly, he was not dressed in black.

"Maybe it's your mom's boyfriend," Jason whispered. Sarah tossed a sarcastic grimace in Jason's face and dug her nervous fingers into his shoulders. Jason took a deep breath and opened the door.

The man standing on the landing was short and plump and appeared quite elderly. He was hunched over with a wooden cane in hand and dressed in a maroon colored argyle sweater-vest and dark green corduroy pants. Coupled with the man's snow white hair and beard he looked like Santa Claus, cherubic face an all. He arched his neck to look Jason in the eye and smiled brightly. "Good day, sir!" the man chimed with a brittle voice as he stretched his shaky, age-spotted hand to Jason.

"Hello," Jason replied in a friendly tone while taking a step forward to engage in a handshake.

The man cleared his throat and began, "May I come in, lad? My name is Dr. Reginald Graystar, and I urgently need to talk to you." Jason responded with a surprised look on his face, not knowing how to vocally reply.

"Me? You are here to talk to me? Not Nadine?" The old man nodded while Jason looked around behind him, examining for possible men in black lurking in the area. He didn't notice any men in black, but he did notice there was not a car awaiting from which Dr, Graystar had arrived.

"How did you get past the guard?" Jason inquired suspiciously.

The man responded quickly, "I came in a cab and told the guard that my speaking with you was a matter of emergency." Jason aided the slow-stepping Dr. Graystar inside the front door and then into the living room so he could sit down.

"Did you try calling earlier today?" Jason questioned.

Dr. Graystar continued to hobble across the marble tile and into the living room, answering Jason's question with a firm, "No."

As he huffed and puffed, Dr. Graystar began to address Jason and Sarah with acute sternness, "I must be brief." The winded Dr.

Graystar hastily walked toward an armchair in the lavish room and sat down with much difficulty. "I am here to help you. You can trust me. I am not part of the men in black organization, but I do know much about them and I also know the two of you, Mr. Morely and Miss Pringle, are facing grave danger. I would like to explain more but we must go somewhere safe and we need to go immediately. We have no time to waste. I'm sorry to burden you with such news but I urge you with everything in my being that if you want to remain alive you must do as I say." Jason and Sarah stared at the old man in bewilderment as he breathed heavily.

"Why should we trust you?" Sarah stammered, "The men in black said they wouldn't harm us either but they have tried." Sarah confidently confronted the Doctor, showing she wasn't afraid. He did not reply, but instead began to rise to walk away. He finally paused and turned back toward Sarah.

"Before we leave, we need to take your tracker out." Dr. Graystar pointed toward Sarah's hand, then turned to address Jason, "Mr. Morely, you have a tracker too, but I can't be certain as to where. We will have to figure that out later. Right now, you need to believe what I say. Your lives depend on it. You don't have a choice."

A rumble in the distance caught everyone's attention as the man ceased to speak. It sounded like a loud motor of some sort but also with an eerie, high-pitched vibration.

"They're here." Dr. Graystar stood up and tossed his cane aside. He began walking at a much more quick and agile pace than he had been previously. Jason and Sarah followed him from room to room as he drew all the curtains closed and eventually pulled a large butcher's knife from the block in the kitchen. The man who had had such a matter-of-fact, calm demeanor, now seemed frenzied and anxious.

Amidst the chaos, Jason peered outside a small window and saw several men in black approaching the home with machine guns. They were blatant and unfettering in their stance. The men were slowly closing in on the house. At this point, Sarah didn't know where her mother was and began calling to her, shrieking loudly in panic. Without hesitation, Dr. Graystar firmly grasped Sarah's wrist and led her to the sink where he hurriedly gripped the knife and stabbed it into Sarah's hand. As blood began to pool and her muscles started to jerk, the Doctor began to cut. She let out a soft, surprised yelp as she felt the warm blood run down her fingers and drop delicately into the sink. For such an old man, he was incredibly strong, holding Sarah's wrist with such might that she could barely move at all. All she could do was wince in agony, trying not to focus on the pain.

Jason entered the room to gaze upon the bloody scene. "What the hell is going on? What are you doing?" Jason defensively approached Dr. Graystar as if to fight him. The exasperated man turned his head to Jason, but continued to cut at Sarah's hand with an unflinching grip.

"Mr. Morely, please, I am doing this for your protection…hers too." He looked back down at Sarah's hand and continued to cut the flesh. The little black dot between Sarah's thumb and index finger had in fact been a tracking device the whole time.

Dr. Graystar, through this savage and painful act, was showing his true intent to help the young couple, and his protection was beginning to get noticed. Sarah, whimpering, placed her other hand on Jason's back to calm him down. Jason stepped away and quickly spun around to find Nadine in the entryway. She was only seconds away from fainting after witnessing the carnage occurring in her kitchen sink. Jason ran to catch her as she rigidly collapsed to the floor.

A blood-covered Dr. Graystar wrapped Sarah's hand in a towel after completing the excision. The small, black cylinder had not been a freckle at all. Sarah rushed over to Jason and her mother while Dr. Graystar quickly washed his hands and stomped firmly atop the thin, tubular tracking device before putting it down the sink's powerful garbage disposal.

While Jason tended to Nadine who was coming to, Sarah approached Dr. Graystar, but her attention was quickly averted to shadows that were appearing through the window's sheer curtain.

She slowly and discreetly peered outside to see a large team of men in black still congregating at the gated entrance below. Observing the assembly himself, Dr. Graystar announced, "We need to get out of here. Is there any way to escape this house without being detected? I fear I have come too late."

Everyone stood to their feet and Nadine replied wearily, "There is an underground passage through the wine cellar, but it only leads to the inside of the back gate. If the entire gate is surrounded, we will be seen trying to get out that way." Jason helped to stabilize Nadine as she spoke.

Dr. Graystar sighed, "It may be the only option we have." After a short pause while everyone pondered their escape, Nadine perked up a bit and said, "I can have Maxwell, my driver, meet us back there so we can jump into the car and go. We will have to climb the gate, but it is not too high." Dr. Graystar smiled. "Excellent. No time to waste." Nadine frantically punched numbers into her cellular phone to call Maxwell. As she arranged the car, Nadine, Sarah, Jason and the Doctor all began to make their way to the wine cellar.

The cellar was filled with rows and rows of racked wine bottles from floor to ceiling. Nadine had to lead the way since the large area felt like a giant maze that only someone who frequented such twists and turns could navigate. No one even noticed that as they continued vertically past more and more wine that they were no longer in the cellar but inside a well-lit tunnel. As they finally reached the back door, Nadine was able to look out a small peephole to peer around. She could see the black SUV Maxwell had parked discreetly below a gathering of pine trees. She could also see at least three armed men in black looking around and chatting through inconspicuous earpiece and speaker sets.

"They're everywhere, inside the gate, surrounding the house," Nadine whispered.

Dr. Graystar looked to Jason and began to softly inform him, "You may not have developed your powers as much as I know you are capable, but I need you to concentrate and create a diversion or a way that we can move the length from here to the car undetected."

Jason, ready to object, speedily thought of an idea. Maybe he could use his mind to make something happen, but how would he know if it had worked or not?

Everyone waited in silence, fearful and tired chests heaving with each passing second. Jason closed his eyes, concentrated, and in a couple of moments, a loud explosion could be heard on the opposite side of the house. The ground shook beneath them, almost taking Nadine to her knees. Dr. Graystar looked out the peephole and beckoned the others to prepare to run.

"They are running toward the sound. Hurry! Run! Go! Now!"

Everyone plunged from the doorway to the rolling grass hill and ascended the small valley from the cellar toward the trees the car was parked next to. With what seemed remarkably dexterous and skillful, everyone got over the fence rapidly and easily. They loaded into the parked SUV and Nadine shouted at Maxwell.

"Drive fast! Quickly! Take us to…" Nadine looked at Dr. Graystar with inquiry. "Where to?"

Mr. Graystar positioned himself toward Maxwell and asked, "Are you familiar with the Darkhill Caves area?"

Maxwell thought and quickly replied, "No sir." Dr. Graystar urged Maxwell to drive South from their current location and he would navigate him as they went.

"You must be fast, Maxwell," the Doctor urged, "It won't be long before our escape is noticed and they will start looking for us. Jason, you need to stop using your power from this moment forward until I let you know it is safe."

Again, the team fell silent while trying to make sense of the confusing chaos that was currently taking place. Sarah finally broke the silence.

"How did you do that, Jason? What did you do?" Jason mustered a half-hearted smile before replying.

"I wasn't sure what I was doing but I wanted it to look like a bomb went off. I figured the men in black would run toward the noise to investigate, plus I determined that it would produce a cloud of smoke and debris to further cover our escape." Jason was proud of the feat he had just accomplished, knowing he had, for that moment at least, saved everyone's life. After pondering the blast, Jason spoke aloud, "Maybe the men in black think we died in the blast. Who knows?"

Dr. Graystar shook his head and explained, "What you did was brilliant, Mr. Morely, but I guarantee they know at least you are alive. Believe me when I say everyone here is expendable, everyone except you." Silence again. Dr. Graystar continued as the SUV drove further from town and into the desert.

"They know you are alive because you have a type of tracking device implanted inside you. It is similar to what Miss Pringle had in her hand, but you can only be tracked when your power is being used, hence why I need you to not use your powers until I tell you that you are safe to do so." Sarah took Jason by the hand and began examining them.

"It won't be in his hand," Dr. Graystar declared, "It would most likely be deeper into the skin, perhaps beneath a bone or embedded in a muscle. It is not something you could detect by sight."

Jason stared Dr. Graystar deep into his eyes, and with a bout of courage demanded, "How do you know all this? Who the hell are you? Where are you taking us? How do we know that what you are saying is even true?"

Sarah patted Jason on the back in a gesture to soothe his anger. Dr. Graystar was eager to answer.

"I'll start by saying that I am an expert in the field of UFO and extraterrestrial history and phenomena. I've been studying these events for the last forty years after having my own MIB encounter. I have learned about who they are, what they want and how they are executing their plans." Nadine looked pale and ill, unable to fathom the truth that was being revealed. She tried to compose herself, sitting cross-legged with good posture, but it didn't take long before she interrupted the conversation.

"I don't know what is going on. If this is a joke or whatever this is, I want no part. I told you Sarah that this boy was a bad seed. People are after you, an old man is cutting your hand in my kitchen sink, and then a bomb goes off. I mean, I'm happy we are safe right now, but whatever you are really involved in, whatever this code wording for extraterrestrials and UFOs and men in black, I don't want any part of it. I demand to be taken to the country club immediately. Sarah, I advise you come with me and get away from Jason and…whoever this old fool is. They are both clearly insane!" Nadine was very fired up and angry at this point, flailing her arms and turning red in the face, but Sarah was not going to provide the solace her mother desired. Instead, she snapped back at Nadine.

"Mother, this is Dr. Graystar and I think you are being very impolite. Don't you realize he just saved our lives! Think what you want, go where you want, but Jason and I are in grave danger, maybe you too. We need to stay with Dr. Graystar and give him a chance to explain whatever is happening to us!" Nadine crossed her arms and discharged an infuriated huff.

"I am perplexed at whatever this nonsense is. Please get out of my car now. I'll have Maxwell drop you off here and you can find a rental or a taxi…I need some time to myself to relax after this incredibly tumultuous day. You may return to my house tonight if you need a place to sleep, but please, get the rest of this craziness out of your systems."

Nadine ordered Maxwell to hastily usher all the passengers from the car. She bid them farewell at the nearest rental car station that had serendipitously been located across the street from where she had announced for everyone to get out. Without leaving time for anyone else to utter a word, Maxwell hit the pedal, and Jason, Sarah, and Dr. Graystar looked at each other with speechless expressions.

Dr. Graystar finally gathered the courage to inquire, "Your mother is quite forward, isn't she, Miss Pringle?" Sarah shook her head in embarrassment, not needing to answer the question verbally.

The Doctor beckoned the group forward into the rental car station. "We need an all-terrain type vehicle. A big van or something. We need to go to the Earthlands." Jason and Sarah exchanged suspicious glances at each other, pressing forward while trying to forget Nadine, her outbursts, and her doubt.

The Earthlands Dr. Graystar was referring to was an area outside the city that was comprised of rolling sand dunes intertwined with cavernous rocky cliffs, ridges, and caves. The area is a mix of conflicting elements that merges the cold rock formations from ancient glacier-covered areas with hot, arid desert flatlands. It was an area popular for a few things: hiking and off-roading excursions, getting away from bustling city life to live like a hermit or to go camping, and of course, it is a notorious area for UFO sightings. The area was also vast, therefore leaving many people unwilling to deeply explore its expanse in too much detail considering the possible dangers.

Dr. Graystar, as they entered the vehicle they rented with Jason driving, navigated the team as he explained where they were going.

"I have an office in the Earthlands, Darkhill Caves area. The coordinates are N. 33°10' 48.319" and W. 112° 17' 55.726". It's a cave alright, well-hidden, but it's where I work, sometimes even live for lengthy periods of time while doing my research."

Sarah sat forward in the backseat, bringing her ear closer to Dr. Graystar's voice.

She interrupted him with a quick question, "Just exactly what type of doctor are you?"

Dr. Graystar chuckled to himself, "I'm a neuroscientist. I study the brain, but my real passion is understanding life, life forms, and unexplained phenomenon. Have you heard of dark matter?" Sarah and Jason both responded that they had heard of it. "It's probably not what you think," the Doctor continued, "anyway, it's beside the point. I'm here to help you both not only from danger but also to aid you in your understanding of the power Jason possesses."

Dr. Graystar babbled on for over an hour as he navigated Jason through sandy, barren roadways. He was vague in his mission, but talked feverishly about what people do not understand about aliens, cosmic energies, UFOs, hoaxes, conspiracies, and other extraterrestrial phenomena.

The ride seemed endless and bumpy, Sarah feeling her stomach turn queasy with each winding turn and mound. Finally, after three hours, the last left turn placed the trio and the vehicle in a small canyon with a cave-like entrance centered amongst the bottom of an enormous sand dune. As the dust began to settle, Sarah and Jason exited the car to find a spry Dr. Graystar jaunting toward the cave entrance with no limp, hobble, or assistance of a cane. Jason and Sarah gave each other a perplexed glance. It was as if he had feigned being feeble while at Nadine's house when he strode with what seemed to be great difficulty. Dr. Graystar turned to beckon the two inside. Everyone ducked as they entered the cave and walked a few feet underground along a dark corridor. The red sand had turned into a dark blackish maroon color, as if it were wet. Sarah stuck a hand out to feel the wall. It was hard like stone but textured like grains of sand. Once deeper inside, Dr. Graystar lit a series of lanterns that looked like they had been part of ancient history. As the light illuminated the area, Sarah and Jason saw that they were inside a gigantic circular room with a large rectangular desk set in the middle that was covered in papers. Many enormous bookshelves lined the outer perimeter of the room. They were overflowing with all sorts of books, manuscripts, scrolls, maps, and loose-leaf papers. There were a few leather chairs that adorned the table that were also covered in papers. Sarah and Jason stood bewildered at the sight as Dr. Graystar continued to hastily light lanterns to brighten the room.

"What is this place?" Jason asked in a whisper. "Welcome to my office," Dr. Graystar replied. Moving papers around and begging to forgive the mess, Dr. Graystar had Sarah and Jason sit down and make themselves comfortable.

"I've allowed you to come here because of the danger the two of you are facing. You are both the first people to ever set foot in this secret place other than myself…at least what I know of." He continued to speak, not allowing for any interruption. "This place inside the Earthlands, my office as I call it, has been an ancient and secretive place for thousands of years. From my research, the caves that envelop this area are known collectively as the Darkhill Caves, and this cave in particular is named Luna Cave. I have been able to continue to keep this place a secret because I don't utilize any sort of technology. From what I have learned, the aliens, these men in black, anyone who is after you is using technology to track you and find you. Right now, the energy of this place blocks out the capability of technology to penetrate these walls. I also never do anything that could possibly infiltrate the area. I don't use a computer or cell phone down here. I also don't use electricity as you can see. I often stay here for days or even weeks at a time and I have dedicated the last four decades of my life studying extraterrestrial life and primarily the motivations of the men in black."

Sarah grabbed at Jason's hand. They both knew they were involved in something much more immense than their minds could ever imagine. Jason pleaded and proclaimed that he was of no value to the men in black and that they should just simply leave them all alone. Dr. Graystar began to pace the rutted dirt floor, trying calmly to explain.

"I must tell you everything, for your protection and for the sake of your future survival. It's going to be a lot of information and an historical account, but you must listen to every word and take to heart that everything I say is true and accurate. Nothing is fabricated, embellished, or fantasized, no matter how absurd or impossible it may sound. I beg that you listen carefully and seriously. I am the only person on the face of planet earth as I know that can help you. I have risked my own life and have prepared my entire life, researched voraciously for decades, all for this very moment. I knew one day I would have to be here, in this position, aiding the two of you, two very normal human beings, against an intergalactic war. Are you ready to listen?"

CHAPTER 9

Jason and Sarah gripped their hands tighter. There was an uncertainty in their minds, but there was not an ounce of jest in the old man's tone. The two nodded, mouths agape, waiting to hear Dr. Graystar begin his story.

"For many millennia, as far back as we have lived, humankind has doubted and speculated that alien life forms have existed. Nothing has ever been definitive, but many philosophers and learned men have at least felt somehow that humans are not the only intelligent living beings on earth or any other planet. To believe that almost seems silly. Why would a vast universe, unexplored fully by humans, the most advanced and intelligent of creatures as has ever been recorded, be utterly empty despite one planet? It has been argued of weather, climate, terrain, food, anatomy, and sense that makes other areas of space uninhabitable, but that argument can only be proven if all other life forms, whether real or imagined, were also comprised of mostly human characteristics…"

Dr. Graystar unfolded his hands and continued to pace the floor. He continued the story before Jason or Sarah could ask questions.

"You don't need a full history lesson here, but I am positive that alien life forms exist. You can call them whatever you'd like…

aliens, martians, extraterrestrials, cosmic beings…there are many of them that inhabit all planets and some are characteristically human while others look like single-celled blobs. However, almost all species and races of aliens are more advanced and intelligent than human beings. In particular, there is a species of alien called Armikkan. They inhabit several planets and galaxies, but their most homogenized locale is on the planet Venus. They don't look like aliens from the movies with long fingers and big heads and green skin. They actually have quite human-appearing qualities. They have a translucent, white skin that can vary to a light gray hue, which usually occurs as they age. They can be tall or short, fat or skinny, but the average build is tall and thin. There are no genders. They have eyes and lips and ears, very similar to our human features, but oftentimes they do not value hygiene or appearance the same way humans do. All Armikkan can reproduce asexually, and sexuality is not an attribute of the species. Family, however, is a big deal, which is why Armikkan like to reproduce over and over and over. I estimate that their populous is now in the millions. However, the gestational period of an Armikkan alien is thirty years, and their life span is typically up to 1,000 years. They also adhere to rules, law, and a form of government.

"The Armikkan population has overtaken all other alien life forms except humans. Unfortunately, the Armikkan, however devoted to family and the continuation of their race, hates humankind. They believe us to be an entity set on destroying the universe rather than conserve and enjoy it. They feel Earth has been decaying slowly, to the point that in the last two centuries it has impacted the surface of Venus's terrain. Many Armikkan have had to flee and relocate to avoid the harm being done on Venus.

"Another species that has become quite large is an alien race called the Periyondy. They are almost indistinguishable in appearance from Armikkan, yet they are entirely different. They are more human in their characteristics with fleshier skin and internal organs similar to ours. They have male and female genders, sexual ideologies, emotions far more complex than that of the Armikkan, and they also age the same way as humans do. They feel a connection to humans, and they are the aliens humans cans attribute to the documented sightings and understanding of extraterrestrial phenomena. Periyondy, however, are exceedingly intelligent and savvy with advancing their species. The Armikkan also dislike the Periyondy because of their intelligence and ability to command themselves and humankind…"

Dr. Graystar drew in a breath while Jason and Sarah took everything in.

"Yes, you heard me correctly, the Periyondy can control humans. People like me who have studied and deciphered and attempted to understand them don't know why the Periyondy can control us, but we do know they have only targeted a small amount of humans in varying different ways. Jason, you have been implanted with a type of device by a Periyondy alien. May I ask, have you ever had a serious surgery?"

Jason glanced at Sarah awkwardly, then back at Dr. Graystar.

"Yes I have. I fell from a tree when I was nine years old. I broke my skull open and was in the hospital for thirty-seven days. I underwent several surgeries."

Sarah tried not to interrupt but couldn't hold in her wonderment.

"Jason, you never told me about that!" Jason laughed anxiously.

"Yeah, I don't really tell anyone. I keep my hair this way to cover the scar. I don't like to talk about those days. I was in a coma for a week and it was the scariest thing I can hardly remember if that makes sense."

Dr. Graystar urged the couple to relax while he began to boil water in a tea kettle. The burst of flames from the hearth gave the element of surprise and seemed to aid in the suspense of the story. Dr. Graystar continued to speak while setting up mismatched tea cups and saucers.

"That injury was when you were implanted. It wasn't an accident. You didn't know it, but those fragmented memories from your coma…that was when the Periyondy grafted a tracking device inside you. They didn't take your body anywhere or physically touch you at all. They visited you in your mind, and implanted you in an unexplainable way, somehow crossing the space-time barrier. I'm just not sure how they did it, but nonetheless, I am certain of this time being the beginning." Jason's hand shot up, asking indirectly for Dr. Graystar to stop for a moment.

"Why would they want me? What was this the beginning of? I just don't understand this stuff, Doc. When was Sarah implanted?" Jason waited for the answers with anticipation.

"You are a weapon, Jason." Dr. Graystar said it slowly and dramatically so it would sink in.

Jason's face crinkled with disbelief, but he finally managed to whisper, "A weapon for what?"

Dr. Graystar chuckled nervously but continued, "Let me answer the rest of your questions first." He continued the story after clearing his throat.

"A long time ago, longer in time than you can fathom, a race of aliens called the Dallkine accidentally discovered an energy, a sort of dark matter if you will, that was so powerful that it could literally control everything on earth. It could create life or destroy it. The legend says that shortly after the energy's birth, it was deemed too dangerous, and subsequently, it was destroyed. The aliens launched the energy in an impenetrable shell from a firing beam billions of light-years into uninhabited space where it would never be found. However, one greedy Dallkine alien is said to have collected a tiny speck of the energy before its launch into a space capsule. This alien sold the energy for a planet of his own, one that humans are still unaware of but the written texts call it Futurra. This transaction resulted in the high ranking Periyondy having ownership of the speck of energy.

"Once word spread throughout the galaxies that the Periyondy owned a speck of the energy, the Armikkan became hell-bent on claiming the energy for their own. The energy was bound to make its owner the most powerful governor of all space and time. However, the Periyondy knew the Armikkan would not use the energy for good if they were to possess it. This enraged the

Armikkan and fueled a war between them and the Periyondy. It is a war that still lingers today and may never end until one of the species no longer exists.

"The Armikkan have worked tirelessly to find the original energy sample that was sent into deep space, but to no avail. They tried to create the energy themselves, but have not even closely succeeded. The last attempt to obtain the energy was to steal it from the Periyondy. But the Armikkan's plans were thwarted, and the energy was taken by a Periyondy elder disguised as a human to Earth where it was to be implanted into a human being for safekeeping. It is estimated that the first human to have been implanted with the power began around the year 1425 and has been re-implanted time and time again after the human's life has ended. Certain Periyondy have now become guardians of these humans who are given the power. You know them as the men in black. They are actually aliens guarding the power from being stolen or discovered."

This time Sarah interrupted with anger in her voice, "But they tried to kill Jason! The men in black are no guards!" Dr. Graystar shook his head.

"No, my dear. The good ones are Periyondy. The bad ones, the men in black who tried to kill Jason, those were Armikkan. They have discovered how to pose as men in black in an attempt to find the human host and obtain the energy. That is who wants you dead…Armikkan!"

"No way! This cannot be happening to me for real." Jason stood up, hands on hips, pacing with disbelief in what he was hearing. It was becoming too much to take in.

With complete seriousness, Dr. Graystar spoke loud and clear for Jason to understand the gravity of the situation.

"It's to the point where it is too late now, Jason. Armikkan MIB and Periyondy MIB know the energy's host is you. They know because you are the first host in history to have tuned into the power and have been able to use it."

Jason scoffed, still bewildered. He shouted frantically, "All I really did was levitate, make stuff fall, open a few doors. It's never been anything that could be considered that big of a deal. Now I'm being hunted for something I really don't have control over?"

Dr. Graystar paused long before he answered, "Yes. You can control it though. You just don't know it yet." The Doctor walked over to Jason and planted his hands firmly on Jason's shoulders as if to hold him in place.

"This power allows you to anything and everything you could imagine. You could kill every living thing from here to the end of the darkest part of the furthest universe. You can go into the future, turn back time, even time travel. You can read minds, walk through walls, become invisible, or turn everything you touch into gold. You can do anything…"

Jason pulled away and responded, "As cool as all that sounds, I just want to get rid of it. I never really used it for good anyway. It was mostly just fun and games."

Dr. Graystar pondered, "We can certainly do what we can to rid you of the power, but you now also have an obligation for the power to not fall into the wrong hands. If that happens, the energy can destroy everyone and everything. Your life isn't the only thing that hangs in the balance. It's everyone's life…"

The teakettle whistled loudly and began to bubble over. Sarah blinked astonished as if she had just come out of a daze. Jason jumped in fear as if a shiver had come over his entire body. As Dr. Graystar calmly served the tea, Jason whispered, "So what do I do now?"

CHAPTER 10

Everyone tried to drink their tea, hoping it would soothe their spirits. Dr. Graystar, after taking a large gulp, rose himself up and walked over to a bookshelf where he took down a large ledger by its binding.

"This is my research from the past forty years. I've been meticulous about keeping notes pertaining to extraterrestrial events, sightings, species, genealogy, men in black, and of course, the bit I do know about this energy you have within you." Dr. Graystar set the open ledger in front of Jason where he noticed the entirety of its thousands of pages were hand written. Jason briefly thumbed a few pages where there were many written words and sketches, almost like Leonardo Da Vinci's notebook.

Dr. Graystar gazed upon both Jason and Sarah and queried, "Remember how when we met I was walking with a cane and a limp?" Both Sarah and Jason nodded in unison. "I did that because the aliens like to prey upon those who seem weak. I thought perhaps if we got into trouble the men in black that were after you would turn to me first instead of you, Jason. I mean, I do value my life and of course I couldn't let all this research go to waste. I was aware and prepared that the day would come that the human host for the Periyondy would discover the power. They believe humans lack intelligence to hone in on such power, but I knew it would happen eventually. I just wasn't sure when or how. The problem now lies in the fact that the Armikkan know the secret to where the Periyondy have been hiding the energy all these centuries…the one place the Armikkan would never come to look. Earth is a place the Armikkan hate and rarely come to tread. What we need to do is get the capsule out of your head and give it back to the Periyondy."

Sarah stood quickly and walked around to examine the ledger. She spoke softly, "Why don't we just destroy the energy?" Dr. Graystar gave Sarah a weary expression.

"I wish it were that simple. This energy cannot be destroyed, and even if we could, it's not ours to destroy. We are all in the middle of the largest, deadliest, and longest extraterrestrial war that has ever been known to occur. We are not even capable of fathoming those facts. We must not insert humankind into this warfare, even if we have been the unknowing vessels carrying the energy for all this time in secrecy."

Jason touched his head, wondering if he could feel something beneath the scalp for tangible proof. "Why me? Was I just a random host?" Dr. Graystar tried to answer the question with care, hoping that Jason and Sarah were not completely scared away by all that they had just heard.

"You were not randomly chosen, Jason. You were chosen by design."

Now Jason found the whole thing beginning to sound too farfetched. "So I'm like a robot? What the hell!" Dr. Graystar kept his cool, but was stern in conveying the significance in his attitude. "No. You are human, Jason. However, a leader of the Periyondy, a highly intelligent extraterrestrial being, carefully selected you based on your human traits. I'm not sure what about you made them choose you, but it could have to do with your intellect or your personality. I would hypothesize that the Periyondy leader decides the human host based upon who they think would be the most unassuming and the most unlikely to discover the energy within them. Unfortunately for you, the meeting of you and Sarah together was the catalyst that sparked the energy into full force. Your attraction to each other must have brought it out." Jason and Sarah smiled at each other, knowing the love they shared was mutual, but they were both also still behind in processing all the information Dr. Graystar had been unleashing. The Doctor continued regardless.

"What most people don't realize is that if we try hard enough, tap into our brains in areas not often used, anyone can emit a similar power to some degree…anyway, I'll get to the point as quickly as possible. The fix to this problem is not an easy one, but my research makes me feel confident in the outcome. Since you are the first of humankind to discover and utilize this power, there is no exact knowledge behind what will happen. The risk is certainly plausible." Dr. Graystar was trying to keep Jason and Sarah comfortable but he knew what he was about to say was going to be unsettling.

"We are going to have to contact a Periyondy elder to remove the implant in your brain."

Sarah interrupted, "And that will take all his powers away?" Dr. Graystar glimpsed at Jason who was studiously waiting for the doctor's reply.

"Yes. The powers will go away." Jason beamed, ready to take action.

"What are we waiting for? Let's get this thing started." Dr. Graystar held out his hand as Jason started for the exit, signaling for him to stop.

"This isn't going to be fast or easy, Jason. I just want you to prepare yourself." The Doctor said nothing more as he headed for the door. Jason and Sarah followed, anxiously awaiting the next move. The trio got back into the rental car. Jason drove as Dr. Graystar gave instructions for him to follow. The car was heading deeper into the crags and dunes of the Earthlands. Panic and fear coursed through Jason and Sarah's mind. Everything was real, which meant they would knowingly be coming face to face with an alien if Dr. Graystar was correct. The ride through the desert lingered in shared silence, but each occupant's mind was screaming in thought.

About thirty miles in, Dr. Graystar pointed to a lone dune with a large, round boulder settled at its bottom and said, "There." Jason drove a bit closer before parking the dust-covered car in front of the boulder. While exiting the vehicle, a chill swept over Sarah. The sun was beginning to set and a light breeze made the area much cooler in temperature than it appeared. Dr. Graystar did not take the time to enjoy the weather or the view. Instead, he jaunted over to the enormous rock that stood about two feet taller than he. Jason and Sarah began to stare in wonderment as Dr. Graystar worked his way to the back side of the boulder, eventually fading from view. Within moments, he returned with a large metal box with wires and antennas plunging from the top. It appeared to be heavy, but Dr. Graystar maneuvered the strange contraption with ease. He walked closer to the car where Jason and Sarah remained standing and set the device on the ground in front of them. They watched with curious eyes as the doctor began tugging and manipulating the different pieces of metal.

As he continued, Dr. Graystar explained, "This rig here is an invention of mine. I call it *The Communicator*. It's a device used to contact aliens. I've had very little success in the past, but I think this time a Periyondy will definitely come to claim the power. I'm sure of it. I need Jason to stand near it, but Sarah, would you kindly back away a bit as I get it ready to signal." Sarah obeyed. Dr. Graystar finished positioning the contraptions' many parts and then drew out a keyboard from the bottom that attached like one on a computer would. He started to type feverishly as a long message began to appear on a translucent colored paper that seemed thin and flimsy, almost as if it were some sort of special cling wrap. The words were very small, but the ink was shiny and fluorescent in color and shone vibrantly as the sun sank deeper into the desert horizon.

Dr. Graystar continued to type furiously while simultaneously explaining what he was doing.

"I am typing a message to the Periyondy elder in charge to find our location and come to meet with us. I am not going to say anything about the power, as I don't know if the message can be intercepted by others, most notably the Armikkan. However, I am instilling great urgency and importance into the tone of the message."

Sarah chuckled slightly and asked, "How are the aliens going to read it? I imagine they don't speak, read, or write English." Dr. Graystar smiled, but did not draw his eyes away from the message he was still composing.

"Don't underestimate the Periyondy, my dear. They are much more advanced than humankind and are extremely smart. They can translate our language and even dictate back. I've discovered that the Periyondy understand information in sequences of prime numbers. Their alphabet is numbers and the amount of words in a phrase makes up the rhetoric." Sarah's eyebrows shot up with immense astonishment. The idea of another species more advanced than humans still seemed absolute fantasy. The numbers and sequence design seemed like something only Einstein would be able to master.

After keying the final stroke on the keyboard, Dr. Graystar exclaimed, "Ahhh, it's finished! Just like an email it travels at a speed so great that the message will arrive to another planet in about fifteen minutes."

Sarah, still probing the reality of communicating with aliens inquired, "How do you know where to send the message to?"

Dr. Graystar began setting up the *The Communicator* device to receive word back while explaining matter-of-factly, "Like I said, it's very similar to an email. The printing that comes out of the device, this clear plastic material with ectoplasmic ink transfers to a similar device, or at least I imagine it to be, that the aliens can translate. They then send a message in return, translating back into numbers that correspond to the English language so we can understand. It will appear on this same material." Sarah wasn't finished with the interrogation. No matter how scientific he explained it, the current events were absolutely astonishing, if not impossible to fathom.

"How did you invent this device and know it would work?" Dr. Graystar looked up for the first time since beginning the communication attempt and chuckled heartily.

"I made 827 prototypes before this one finally worked. Trial and error, my dear, and, of course, great patience and tenacity." He continued to tinker with the device, Sarah at a loss for words and Jason in great, paralyzing bewilderment.

"It doesn't always work, unfortunately," Dr. Graystar grunted, "but it is the only thing that has worked. We will give it some time and see if we get a response."

CHAPTER 11

The trio had been waiting for forty-five minutes, anxiously awaiting word from a Periyondy alien. Jason was trying to ease his mind as well as Sarah's by throwing pieces of trail mix into each other's mouths to see who could catch the most without using their hands. Sarah had just missed catching a peanut when her attention was averted to a noise emanating from *The Communicator*. Just as the doctor had predicted, the same luminescent ink and clear film began to compose a message. Dr. Graystar hastily approached to read it as Sarah and Jason gathered around. He cleared his throat and began to read aloud for Jason and Sarah to hear.

"It says that the Periyondy leader has received our message and is due to arrive at our location in just a few moments. It says they understand the importance and immediacy of our asking to meet…"

Gazing up into space, Dr. Graystar muttered quietly, "We are all going to meet a real live alien." Not knowing whether to expect a flying saucer to beam down or an army to fall from the sky in special little pods, Sarah hastily got into the back seat of the car. Jason and Dr. Graystar followed suit. Jason could see the fear rising in Sarah's expression. Her hands were lightly trembling and she was holding tightly to her injured hand.

"Don't worry," Jason began, "after all the men in black are aliens and we have been around them all this time. Look at the descriptions of Mr. Diamond and Mr. Spade from the research we've done. They fit the exact descriptions of Armikkan. I'm sure this will be no different. You have nothing to fear. I'll protect you."

Sarah leaned into Jason to give him a warm hug. He felt magical in her embrace, as if everything was going to be okay. Dr. Graystar, however, knew that the meeting with the Periyondy would likely be much easier than many other things Jason and Sarah would have to go through before their ever-changing problems were over.

The sun had finally plunged its last glimmering light below eye view, and total darkness was beginning to spread over the desert. The stars in the sky sparkled brightly, but the trio waited patiently inside the dark car for the next move, unaware of the beauty surrounding them. Jason fidgeted with his hands. Sarah closed her eyes and focused on her breathing. Dr. Graystar kept peering up and down and around, awaiting the Periyondy arrival.

Suddenly, a rapping on the backseat window jolted everyone from their thoughts. Turning on the vehicle's interior light, Jason could see a man standing outside. Dr. Graystar exited the vehicle while Sarah and Jason stood helplessly engaged in their terror. It wasn't until Dr. Graystar and the stranger could be heard engaging in polite conversation that Jason felt it safe enough to check things out. He slowly stepped out the opposite side from where the men were standing, and as he approached he took a better look at the moonlit stranger. He looked human enough, but it was obvious he was out of his element in terms of dress. The man was wearing a dark brown cloak with a gold chain belt, almost like an old fashioned friar's ensemble. He walked with a gnarled wooden cane that appeared as though a thousand splinters would stick into human flesh upon a firm grasp. The man had a dark olive complexion and long, black hair in which tendrils of it filled the hooded cloak. He was tall and thin, but quite a bit bigger overall than a tall and thin human.

Jason stood closer to Dr. Graystar as the two were introduced.

"Jason, meet the Periyondy elder, Clarence. Clarence, meet Jason Morely, your human host." The two men exchanged handshakes and Jason did his best to not divert his eyesight away from the looming man.

"I am very thankful and fortunate to meet with you, Clarence," Jason whimpered uncertainly.

Clarence replied, "It is my honor to be able to meet you in person as well. I know quite a lot about you, Mr. Morely, but I have never come to Earth while you have been the human host." Jason was perplexed by the perfect speech and tone the alien possessed. It almost made one return to the notion that the whole incident was a just an over-the-top hoax. Jason didn't take long to ponder.

Instead he insisted, "So, Clarence, can you just take the implant out or whatever you need to do so I can go back to a normal life?" Silence. Clarence looked at Dr. Graystar, then back to Jason before responding.

"We need to talk in depth about what needs to take place. Removal of the implantation device is risky on a live human and something we have never had to do before. Usually we take it out after the human host has expired and then implant it into another. However, in order to remove it, it will take a similar procedure as how it was initially implanted."

Jason's knees felt weak. He leaned against the car, replaying the moments he could recall from his childhood while he laid in a coma.

"I know this seems difficult, Jason, but if the Armikkan get to you before this extraction, it will be much worse," Clarence insisted. Dr. Graystar nodded. Jason walked over to get Sarah whose face was covered in rarely seen tears.

"I know," she sobbed, "I heard everything." In light of the circumstance and Sarah's obvious angst, she and Clarence weren't properly acquainted. Dr. Graystar felt the ball needed to get rolling immediately and asked everyone to get into the car so they could go back to his office and prepare for the implant removal. As the foursome piled into the car, Sarah and Clarence exchanged greetings. Jason listened to the conversation between them as he headed in the dark night back toward Luna Cave. Swirling sands impaired his vision, but the Doctor knew the area well and kept him on track. For the most part, the car ride was silent and filled with a tense anxiety.

CHAPTER 12

Dr. Graystar set up a folding cot that appeared to be an old military type with green fatigue mattress covers. Clarence unfolded several white linen cloths that were smaller than bed sheets, but larger than napkins, and placed them atop the mattress. Jason and Sarah watched silently as the other two scrambled about as if preparing for a séance to summon a ghost. They fashioned many large candles about the room and surrounding the cot. Clarence began sprinkling some sort of astral dust around the room, mostly in the area encompassing the cot. Jason easily deduced that he would be the one to lie upon it.

Trying to ease the tension, Jason asked, "May I ask if Clarence is really your name?" The Periyony elder remained expressionless and continued his ritual without answering.

"I think it's probably just a human name," Dr. Graystar whispered, "humans can't comprehend their language, so it is most likely that he issued himself a name that would relate to the human world." Dr. Graystar winked at Jason as he set up some small copper saucers no larger or deeper than a pair of castanets.

"Please, Jason," Clarence uttered, "you must come lie down upon this bed. I will perform the ceremony, enter your mind, and extract the implant containing the power. You will remain in a coma for three earth days while I perform this operation."

As Jason began to comply, Sarah stamped wildly at the idea. "No way!" Everyone's head turned in Sarah's direction awaiting an explanation. "I trust you know what you're doing, but you cannot keep a human in a coma for three days without medical supervision, a hospital, a sterile area. Candle wax and desert dust aren't exactly safe for this sort of thing. Please, Clarence, Dr. Graystar, take him to a hospital...for safe measure."

Clarence protested with pragmatism that going to a hospital would aid in the ability for the Armmikan to find Jason while the operation was under way. Jason, not answering for himself in the least, listened as Sarah vehemently stood firm on the necessity to be close to medical care. Dr. Graystar had to approach her and put a guiding hand atop her shoulder.

"I know this is scary. I know it seems to defy logic, but Jason is in safe hands here. A hospital would be a dangerous place to go. I'm afraid your wishes are limited here to what is possible." Sarah walked away speechless, trying not to be rude but understanding of what was at stake and what needed to be done. The thought of Jason dying was in the forefront of her mind, beginning to make her head ache with an apprehensive agony. She walked around into an alcove away from view of the trio preparing the ritual so she could be alone with her thoughts. Sarah had had all she could stand at this point. Anger, fear, and irritation began to consume her in a way that was physical instead of just emotional. "Just breathe." Sarah quietly began to coax herself, almost to ease the strain and focus on something more uplifting. She would have three days to endure if the procedure to extract the power went as planned. She knew now was not the time to show weakness or think grim thoughts.

Sarah closed her eyes tightly, wincing a moment before redirecting her energy to focus on positivity...or nothing. Nothing felt good. Nothing felt incredible. As her mind went blank, she found relief sweeping over her and then nothing at all. The moment, however, was fleeting. Eyes still closed, a vision came to her, almost as if watching a movie. Her eyes veering back and forth watched in fast motion as Sarah saw herself, Dr. Graystar, and Clarence rejoicing at the outcome of the procedure. Jason's eyes were open and he lit up with delight, free from the prison of his alien power. As Sarah saw herself bending down to give Jason a kiss, the vision went blank just before their lips touched.

Sarah slowly opened her eyes, blinking in astonishment at what had just occurred. Was it dèjá vu? A premonition? A vivid daydream? Sarah wasn't sure what had happened, but no matter what the vision meant, she finally felt a lasting calmness in the moments and days that lay ahead.

CHAPTER 13

Clarence and Dr. Graystar finished the final prep work for Jason's procedure and were now sitting next to him on folding chairs. Jason, surprisingly bright-eyed and cheery, was lying on the cot partially undressed with a white sheet over him. Clarence had inserted small piles of astral dust into the small depressions of Jason's shoulders. The dust sparkled but was ash black in color. The odiferous scent of tar filled the air and was most definitely being produced by Clarence's ritual dust.

Jason tapped the sides of the cot, his fingers springing up and down beneath the white sheet.

"What happens next?" he questioned as Sarah entered into view. "Where'd you go, Sarah?" Everyone remained quiet for a moment, waiting for the expert to guide them.

"We wait," Clarence replied sensibly. Another moment of silence.

"For what?" Jason's head began to bounce from Clarence to Dr. Graystar to Sarah, waiting eagerly for an answer.

"Sleep." Clarence uttered.

Jason didn't feel like he was going to be able to fall asleep any time soon amidst the excitement taking way. Just as Jason was about to say this, Clarence bent down onto his knees at Jason's side and tilted his head back.

"Close your eyes," Clarence said softly and Jason complied. Clarence had used one of the small copper saucers to make a muddy paste using the astral dust and water. He dipped two fingers into the mixture, bringing up two globs of black, shiny goo. He brought the viscous material close to Jason's face and gently smeared it over his eyelids. The cool substance surprised Jason, making his eyes begin to flutter rapidly as if he was trying to open them but was unable to. He also immediately began to feel his body tingle, the sound of Sarah's questioning voice begin to fade into the distance. He knew instantly the procedure was beginning and that the substance atop his eyelids was acting like an anesthetic putting him to sleep.

Just before Jason was completely out, he had one more thing to do. It wasn't something he had planned. It had just occurred to him, but he knew it was something he needed to do. He drew a fatigued arm up into the air from beneath the sheet, curled his hand into a ball, and outstretched his index finger toward the large pile of papers Dr. Graystar had removed from the table when they first entered the cavern. When his arm dropped, flopped, and hung limply by his side, a single piece of paper located in the middle of the stack jutted out, folded itself into a halfway decent paper airplane, and flew about the room until finally resting gently in front of Sarah's feet.

Astonished, Sarah paused a moment before reaching down and picking it up. She examined the origami and realized the paper was not blank. She unfolded it gently and found a large circle embossed in gold leaf. There were no words or indication of what the circle meant, but somehow Sarah knew exactly what Jason was trying to say. The golden ring was Jason's way of asking her to marry him.

A feeling of joy swept over her as Clarence and Dr. Graystar went back to monitoring their patient. Involuntarily, Sarah's ecstasy made her boast excitedly the word "yes" over and over, hoping that Jason could hear her accepting his proposal. Jason didn't. By this time he was far away in his mind where aliens were beginning to exhume the capsule from his brain. As scary as the situation was, Sarah was able to feel giddy and eager. Her vision had shown her that everything would be alright.

CHAPTER 14

Sarah had been curled into a ball on a worn, leather desk chair covered with a knitted blanket when Dr. Graystar roused her with a gentle pat. Stirring sluggishly, Sarah opened her eyes and took a moment to focus on the Doctor.

He whispered to her, saying, "I just wanted to let you know the procedure is going smoothly." Sarah smiled back at a grinning Dr. Graystar.

"Good to know," Sarah replied as she laid her head back down. The Doctor was intrigued by how calm she was acting since before she had seemed excitable and anxious about meeting Clarence and the idea of inducing a coma to have aliens probe the brain of the one man she had fallen madly in love with. Perhaps she was tired from all the chaos. Perhaps the marriage proposal had fostered an inner tranquility. Whatever it was, Dr. Graystar was glad that everything and everyone was getting along smoothly.

When the third day arrived, Clarence announced that the procedure would be finished soon and that Jason would wake up. Hours passed. Sarah filled the time browsing the ancient tomes in Dr. Graystar's collection and watching Clarence studiously as he continued rituals with energy and astral dust as Jason slept. She took some notes, hoping that one day she would be able to write a book about this incredible experience. Boy, would she have a story to tell.

Afternoon turned to evening and Clarence seemed to tire of the continuous movement and exhaustion of energy in aiding the procedure. By dark, he seemed to change demeanor completely. He fumbled inside his robes as if looking for something very precious. He revealed a small, geometric rock inside his bony, withered palm. The stone was bright green and sparkling, like an emerald.

"Is everything alright?" Dr. Graystar inquired. The questioning sent a jolt into Sarah who now became astute as to what was happening to Jason.

Clarence said nothing as he placed the large gem onto Jason's forehead. The alien chanted in a foreign language, and Jason's skin began to ripple from head toe as if ocean waves were surging inside him. After a few seconds, the shaking stopped and Jason's eyelids began to flutter.

"He's awake!" Dr. Graystar rejoiced. A jovial grin spread across Sarah's face. She bounced with happiness. Clarence, however, looked worried and almost confused.

Jason's lips parted and he tried to speak with a low, raspy tone, "Am I dead?" Clarence breathed a long sigh before answering him.

"No. You are perfectly alive. The procedure was successful, but you didn't wake up as soon as I expected. I was troubled for a moment, but I can confirm the capsule and the power have been extracted without problem and the Armikkan have not found us. However, I must leave with haste. Jason, you must rest. It may not look like much has befallen you, but I assure you, the procedure was very involved."

Dr. Graystar approached to shake Clarence's hand and insisted, "We will take good care of him. Thank you, Clarence. It has been an absolute pleasure knowing you."

Unabashedly, Sarah wrapped Clarence in a tight, thankful embrace. Clarence returned the hug knowing what it meant in the human culture. He then turned to collect his belongings and walked outside.

Jason, who had sat upright on the cot, reached out and shouted, "Wait!" He jumped out from under the sheets in nothing but his underwear and jogged in the direction of Clarence. It was too late. Once outside, Jason could plainly see that Clarence had disappeared and had returned just as mysteriously as he had arrived.

Jason hung his head. He was disappointed that he didn't get a chance to thank Clarence nor get to ask any questions. After walking back inside, he felt a rush of embarrassment befall him as he noticed Sarah and Dr. Graystar staring at his sparsely clothed appearance. He reached for the knit blanket Sarah had used to nap with and wrapped it around his body. Sarah smiled with a teasing wink.

"Did you get my message, Sarah?" he asked. She blushed and walked slowly toward him.

"I did," she playfully admitted. Jason paused a moment waiting for her to continue.

When she didn't say anything, Jason inquired, "And?" Sarah stood on her tiptoes to plant a kiss on Jason's waiting lips. She finally uttered, "And…my answer is yes!"

CHAPTER 15

It took a few days for Jason to feel free from fatigue and any remaining pain. His head had throbbed lightly, and he also felt as if he had suffered a sensation similar to vertigo. By this time, Jason and Sarah had returned to Nadine's home. Dr. Graystar stood by Jason's side, monitoring every detail of his recovery, fascinating over the entirety of the procedure while documenting the after effects.

Sarah was happier than she had ever been before, and while Jason remained laid up on bed rest per Dr. Graystar's orders, Sarah walked about with a bounce in her step and a fulfilled attitude. Jason, perplexed by her demeanor asked, "Why are you so happy? I'm still recovering you know. This isn't all over yet." Sarah beamed as if she hadn't heard a word he said. She went to his bedside and stroked his face. Jason was instantly comforted. A moment of silence passed as Jason seemed to doze off.

Sarah bent down toward him and softy declared, "I know you will be alright. I knew all along that everything would be alright. That's why I've been so happy and unworried. I knew it." Jason's eyes slowly opened and he focused on Sarah's eyes with an expression of confusion and shock. He wasn't sure what she meant.

He muttered a squeakily, "Huh?"

Although the moment had been a private one, Dr. Graystar, who had been standing in the doorway to monitor Jason's progress, interjected before Sarah could continue to speak.

"That's because you had experienced a phenomenon known as precognition."

Dr. Graystar folded his hands together and stood at the foot of the bed. Jason sat up and Sarah took a chair nearby with a look of eagerness. When neither Jason nor Sarah uttered a word, all eyes locked onto the Doctor.

He gestured with palms face up and explained, "You saw the future, Sarah." Jason furrowed his brow and clutched his glasses from the nightstand.

"How could she see the future? I thought I had the power and now the power is gone. I don't understand." Sarah nodded, and her confusion almost showed in her face as fear.

Dr. Graystar continued, "It's an ability all human beings possess. It's just one that most people don't tune into. We have so many parts of the brain that go unused, and yet if we can tap into those areas, the abilities we have are extraordinary. Precognition allows a person to see into the immediate future, sometimes for minutes, hours, or even days. Sarah must have tuned into the area of her brain that allowed her to see that outcome to your procedure, Jason."

The couple sat in astonishment unknowing what to say. The concept seemed so farfetched, yet it explained everything they had just been through.

Jason smiled widely and exclaimed, "So you're telling me that without alien powers or any other extraterrestrial intervention that human beings can have the power to see the future?"

Dr. Graystar took a step forward and assured, "Oh, yes! Among other powers as well. I haven't mastered many of them myself, but it is possible." This time Sarah asked excitedly, "Like what?" The Doctor let out a soft chuckle to the two students and began to explain.

"My research has taught me so very much over the years. Humans are merely just a race of aliens among the vast universal expanse of millions of other races. Our capabilities are more advanced than some species and less advanced than others. Some are skilled with their hands, their words, or their minds. Some are skilled in all and others in nothing but basic survival. Humans have the ability to do many things we cannot logically or scientifically explain, and it's rare when one does discover such abilities that it usually goes unnoticed and unstudied. We could do so much if we wanted to, if only we knew how to make our brains react physically to the abilities we desire. Humans can see the future, visit the past, make things happen that they cannot explain like levitate, miraculously cure themselves or others of disease, arise from the dead…you see what I mean."

With a sense of awe, both Jason and Sarah knew Dr. Graystar was telling the truth and they believed him. Sarah didn't know how she had managed to see into the future, but she was glad she had. Dr. Graystar turned to exit the room pleased with his explanation and the couple's reception.

Before he was out of view, he briefly proposed, "I wouldn't normally share my research publically, but Sarah, if you would like to write a story, you have access to everything I have collected and written. My purpose was to get the information. Jason's purpose was to experience it. Your purpose is to share it with the world. I wholeheartedly believe that." He gave Sarah a quick wink, and shuffled happily down the hallway.

CHAPTER 16

It seemed as though the men in black were no longer showing up randomly, but at this point it was still too early to determine it with absolute certainty. Nadine was also still upset over the ordeal Jason and Sarah had put her through, and she was much less happy about the announcement of the couple's engagement. However, as time passed and the hype from all the crazy events settled and were put behind them, Nadine was able to see that Jason really was a good man. It still took some time to open up to him, but she learned to love him almost as much as her own daughter.

It was only a few months after Jason's extraction that he and Sarah tied the knot. It was a small, intimate wedding ceremony on Nadine's grandiose property. Dr. Graystar stood in as Jason's best man. After the celebration was over, Jason and Sarah quickly acclimated to a more normal life, although it was apparent that things would never be the same. The couple had grown in so many ways and were now unwilling to spend a moment in boredom and repetition nor settle for what they knew was below their reach.

Even though the men in black no longer continued to stalk the couple, Sarah and Jason remained on guard for a lengthy period of time. They continued a long lasting friendship with Dr. Graystar whom they both began to treasure as a father figure. The trio would spend long evenings together. Sarah would cook an elaborate meal while the Doctor reminisced about his experiences and education about aliens and extraterrestrial topics.

Jason moved up in the business at Allen Enterprises and was able to open up socially and artistically. Sarah finally found an opportunity to apply for a job as a journalist. Of course, she had to make a good impression by covering a riveting story. Her first published work was received by some with great speculation, but no one could deny that it presented the world with an incredibly attentive fascination. It was aptly titled, "The Graystar Theory."

www.ingramcontent.com/pod-product-compliance
Lightning Source LLC
LaVergne TN
LVHW020427080526
838202LV00055B/5067